Lodges in the Wilderness

by W. C. Scully

Chapter One.

The Bushmanland Desert—Its Nature and Extent—Desert Travelling—The "Toa."

The world moves rapidly and with increasing momentum. Even regions remote from those communities which the stress of increasing population and the curse of unleisured industrialism send spinning "down the ringing grooves of change," are often so disturbed or overwhelmed by the overflow of what threatens to be an almost worldwide current of morbid energy, that within a strangely short period their character is apt completely to alter and their individuality to become utterly destroyed.

I do not know how the Great Bushmanland Desert has fared in this respect— not having visited it for several years—but if some unlikely combination of circumstances were to take me once more to Aroegas or Koisabies,—to the tiny spring of living water that trickles from the depths and lies like a precious jewel hidden in the dark, narrow cavern at Inkruip,—or to where the flaming, red-belted cone of Bantom Berg glares over the dragon-folds of the dune-devil sprawling at its feet, I should go in fear of finding empty sardine-tins and broken bottles lying among the fragments of prehistoric pottery and flint implements which were but recently the only traces of man to be found in those abodes of solitude.

The Bushmanland Desert is but little-known. A few nomads—some of European and some of mixed descent—hang on its fringe. Here and there ephemeral mat-house villages, whose dwellers are dependent on the sparse and uncertain bounty of the sky, will, perhaps, be found for a season. But when the greedy sun has reclaimed the last drop of moisture from shallow "pan" or sand-choked rock-saucer, the mat-houses are folded up and, like the Arabs, these dwellers steal silently away from the blighting visage of the Thirst King. But the greater portion of Bushmanland may be ranked among the most complete solitudes of the earth. The lion, the rhinoceros, and, in fact, most of the larger indigenous fauna have disappeared from it—with the autochthonous pygmy human inhabitants; nevertheless it is a region full of varied and distinctive interest. The landscape consists either of vast plains, mirage-haunted and as level as the sea,—arid mountain ranges—usually mere piles of naked rock, or immense sand-dunes, massed and convoluted. The latter often change their form and occasionally their location under stress of the violent winds which sweep down from the torrid north.

The tract is an extensive one, probably upwards of 50,000 square miles lie within its limits. It is bounded on the north by the Gariep or Orange River—but as that flows and eddies at the bottom of a tremendous gorge which is cut off from the plains by a lofty, stark range of mountains,—coal-black in colour for their greater extent and glowing hot throughout the long, cloudless day, the traveller seldom sees it. The western boundary is the Atlantic Ocean; the eastern an imaginary line drawn approximately south from the Great Aughrabies Falls to the Kat Kop Range. If we bisect this line with another drawn due east from the coast to the Lange Berg, we shall get a sufficiently recognisable boundary on the south. From the tract so defined must be deducted the small area surrounding the Copper Mines, and a narrow strip of mountain land running parallel with, and about sixty miles from the coast. This strip is sparsely inhabited by European farmers.

THE SHIP OF THE DESERT

The occasional traversing of this vast tract lay within the scope of my official duties. My invariable travelling companion was Field Cornet Andries Esterhuizen (of whom more anon) and a small retinue of police, drivers, and after-riders. We never escaped hardship; the sun scorched fiercely and the sand over which we tramped was often hot enough to cook an egg in. Water, excepting the supply we carried with us, was as a rule unobtainable; consequently we had to eschew washing completely. We often had to travel by night so as to spare the oxen, and as the water-casks usually almost filled the wagon, we then had to tramp, vainly longing for sleep, through long, weary hours, from sunset to sunrise. And after the sun had arisen the heat, as a rule, made sleep impossible.

It was to the more inaccessible—and therefore comparatively inviolate— expanses of this wilderness that I was always tempted to penetrate. Therein were to be found a scanty flora and a fauna—each unusual and distinctive,— composed of hardy organisms, which an apprenticeship from days unthinkably ancient had habituated to their most difficult conditions of existence. If, somewhere near the margin of the great central plain, we happened to cross the track of a vagrant thunderstorm, we would see myriads of delicately-petalled blossoms miraculously surviving, like the Faithful Rulers of Babylon in the Fiery Furnace. On the flank of some flaming sand-dune we would find the tulip-

4

like blooms of the Gethyllis flourishing in leafless splendour. Their corollas were of crystalline white splashed with vivid crimson; deep in each goblet lay the clustered anthers,—a convoluted mass of glowing gold. Is this flower a grail, bearing beauty too ineffable to die, through an arid aeon from one cycle of fertility to another?

Sometimes our course led over tracts of sand—sand so light and powdery that the foot sank into it ankle-deep at every step. Occasionally we crossed high, abrupt ridges of black or chocolate-hued rock, separated from each other by gorges so deep that except at noontide, no sunbeam penetrated them. But usually our course lay across plains, infinite in extent. In the Summer season such were covered with heavy-headed shocks of "toa" grass,—yellow or light green in hue, according to the more or less scanty rainfall. But in Winter all the waving plumes crumbled away, leaving the bases of the tussocks as black as pitch. Where the hills and the plains met, stood groves of immense dragon aloes— some cumbered with nests of the sociable grossbeak—each as large as a hayrick.

The lordly oryx crossed our path; the ungainly hartebeest lumbered away to windward at a pace which made pursuit hopeless; the gazelles of the desert fled before us like thistledown borne on an eddying wind. The roofs of many a city of desert mice sank beneath our footsteps and the horned adder hissed defiance at our caravan from his home at the tussock's base. We crossed the zig-zag track made by the yellow cobra when prowling in the darkness. The plumed ostrich scudded away at our approach, the great bustard of the Kalihari spread his powerful wings and flew forth heavily until he almost crossed the horizon, and the "kapok vogeltje," no bigger than a wren, twittered at us from his seat of cunning on the outside of the simulated snowball which is his nest.

We did not fear the poisoned arrows of the Bushmen, for that strange race which formerly occupied the scenes of our wanderings had long since disappeared from the face of the earth. Within the wide bounds of that tract to which the Bushman gave his name, there existed but two individuals of his race,—an old, withered, toothless man, and a bent and ancient crone. These wraiths, who subsisted on roots, reptiles and insects, still haunted the mountains near Dabienoras, and levied a kind of toll on the very occasional traveller. This took the form of a trifling contribution of tobacco and sugar.

Chapter Two.

Andries Esterhuizen—Silverfontein—The Koeker-Boom—Gamoep— Sand-Grouse—Our Horses—Kanxas—Night in the Desert—Dawn— Heat—The Mirage—Bantom Berg—The Dune-Monster—The Flight of the Oxen.

Andries Esterhuizen had lived all his life on the fringe of Bushmanland. His farm, Silverfontein, which lay a little more than twenty miles from the Ookiep Mines, had been for many years the principal jumping-off place for expeditions to the desert. Andries was a Field Cornet,—an office which empowered him to arrest offenders against the law. He was a typical Boer of the better class. Large-boned and tall, his increased bulk had for several years prevented his doing that which his soud loved above all else,—riding down a herd of oryx. His blue, laughing eyes shone from a ruddy face. His brown beard was streaked with grey. His great fist could have felled an ox; the tempest of his laughter was like the neighing of war-steeds.

Andries sent his ox-wagon to fetch my guns and baggage. Next day I followed in a cart drawn by four strong horses, for heavy stretches of sand had to be crossed before reaching Silverfontein.

On arrival there I met with a hearty welcome. The wagon stood, fully packed, before the farm-house door. The heaviest and most important item of the load was three casks of water, for we were about to enter and encamp in the deadly dune-veld where Thirst is a king who has reigned supreme since the world was young. We meant to storm his strong city and occupy it for a season,—well knowing, however, that we should soon have to retire, leaving his ancient realm unconquered and unspoiled. As we did not mean to be luxurious, our commissariat list only included coffee, sugar, salt and "Boer-biscuits" (a kind of coarse but exceedingly palatable rusk). Of these Mrs Esterhuizen had manufactured enough to fill three immense linen sacks. For meat we should have to depend upon our guns.

The country surrounding Silverfontein was wild and rugged. Long, dyked ridges, foam-tipped with snow-white quartzite rocks, stretched away to infinity, north and south; here and there a naked granite finger pointed to the cloudless sky. On the western side these ridges seemed to break like waves against the enormous bronze-hued bastions of the Kamiesbergen; on the eastward they sank by degrees into the ocean-like expanse of the desert.

Huddled in irregular patches where the dykes sprang from the red sand were the "koekerboome" ("quiver-trees,"—so called because the Bushmen used pithed sections of the boughs as receptacles for their arrows.) These were gigantic aloes of archaic form and immense age. As a rule their height was from fifteen to twenty feet. Their ungainly trunks were cone-shaped, groined and heavily buttressed. The rosette-crowned ends of their dichotomous branches collectively formed a more or less irregular oval. But at one spot, as we crossed the line where the hills ended and the plains began, we noticed some with smooth, slender, white boles rising to a height of nearly sixty feet,—each crowned with a single cup-like whorl of leaves.

Gamoep, where the last water was to be found, lay on the actual edge of the level desert some distance to the south-east of Silverfontein. To reach it involved a long day's trek, for the route was through soft sand. At Gamoep was a permanent spring,—the water of which, although fit for animals, was not quite suitable for human consumption. Alongside the pool which the spring feeds we decided to rest for twenty-four hours, for the oxen had a heavy strain to undergo and we felt it necessary to cover as much as possible of the first part of our journey during the cool hours of night.

We slept soundly after our long tramp. Next morning, as the sun began to soar, sand-grouse in flocks of almost incredible numbers came sweeping in from the desert. The wearied birds alighted a few hundred yards from the pool, and there rested for about ten minutes. Then they arose, swooped down to the edge of the pool for a hurried sip, and sped back whence they came. We shot sufficient of these for our immediate needs.

Late in the afternoon, when the sting had gone out of the sunshine, we drove the oxen to the pool and let them drink their fill. We had brought two horses—my old hunting-horse, "Prince," and another "Swaitland," renamed "Bucephalus," for Hendrick, my after-rider. But the horses had to remain for the present at Gamoep, in charge of Danster, one of our Hottentots. Piet Noona, another Hottentot, and his nephew,—a lad of about twelve years of age, were also left behind for the purpose of taking charge of the oxen when they returned, maddened with thirst, after being released from the yoke at the camping-place under Bantom Berg and the Great Dune, which was our objective.

Shortly before sundown we inspanned and made a start, shaping our course north-east. Soon we had crossed the last rocky ridge,—the boundary separating the hilly country from the plains. The latter were covered with the shock-bearing tussocks of "toa,"—waving plumes at that time bleached to a light-yellow by the ardours of the summer sun. We passed the head of the Kanxas Gorge,—a miniature canyon whose rocky, perpendicular sides contained caves which had been until a comparatively recent date occupied by Bushmen. The walls of these caves shew records of their former inhabitants in the form of black-pigmented script. This consists mainly of groups of short, parallel lines crossed at various angles by lines similar. But neither here nor in any of the haunts of the now-vanished Bushmen I have visited in the north-western areas of the Cape Province, have I seen paintings of men and animals such as are to be found in other parts of South Africa. A spring had existed at Kanxas within the memory of living Trek-Boers. Of this no vestige then remained. Herein lies an additional item of evidence pointing to the ominous conclusion that South Africa is slowly but surely drying up.

Night fell; the primrose-yellow of the "toa" faded to ghostly white; not a breath of wind stirred. Excepting the creak, creak, of the straining yokes not a sound was audible. Day faded from the sky and the cupola of stars seemed to descend around us like a curtain. We walked apart and communed with our individual selves. When by night one enters the door of the desert speech seems banal and incongruous.

At about midnight we outspanned. The oxen were, however, kept tied to the yokes; we meant to take but an hour's rest. The patient cattle laid themselves down at once; an occasional long-drawn sigh being the only evidence of their existence. Anon the flame of our candle-bush fire ascended into the windless air,—straight as a column. Coffee was soon ready and biscuits distributed. After we had eaten and drunk, pipes were lit. Then we threw ourselves prone on the sand and gazed, wrapt, into the glittering folds of the star-curtain.

How unutterably still it was; how ineffably peaceful. The spell of silence still sealed our lips. The world of men—with its fierce and futile struggles, its crowded and ever-changing illusions, seemed but a dream. Could it be that in other regions of that earth, which there seemed so austere, so sinless and so ordered, men were struggling in warren-like cities? For that night, however, the desert was the only reality; there we seemed to have attained Nirvana.

The hour of rest soon came to an end; once more the oxen were yoked and our wagon lumbered on. There was no longer a track to guide us; our wheels drew a double-furrow through soil that had never groaned to the share of a plough forged by mortal hands,—that will never yield a crop sown by man. There were no dangers to dread but snakes; no obstacles to avoid—except an occasional tract, ten to fifteen yards in diameter, which had been undermined by desert mice. Through the crust of such a tract the wagon would have sunk to the axles; accordingly a Hottentot was detailed to walk a few yards ahead and give notice of the fact should a mouse-city lie in our course. We steered neither by the compass nor the stars, not yet by any landmark. It was the instinct of Andries and his desert-bred servants,—that "sense of direction" possessed by men whose perceptions have not been destroyed by civilisation,—which enabled them to steer us, straight as an arrow, towards an unseen objective we should only reach two days later.

A pallid gleam shot through the eastern sky; the stars grew faint; over the blue firmament stole, as it were, a sheen of pearl. Soon the rising moon touched the horizon's rim; as we gazed she soared above it. By the first touch of her level beam-wand, fairy-land was created; the plains, sombre since daylight had departed, became ivory-white to eastward; across their immensity extended a broad strip of silver. This was due to the sheen of the new moonlight on the dew-wet plumes arising from the "toa" tussocks.

As night wore slowly on the deep sand became a weariness. Sleep grew importunate; her fingers pressed down our eyelids and the folds of her trailing robe entangled our lead-shod feet. The moon, after her first majestic soar above the horizon, seemed to climb slower and more slowly towards the zenith. It would have been a luxury to fall prone on the velvet-soft sand and sink at once into dreamless oblivion.

But this might not be; our plan of campaign had been cunningly devised and had to be strictly adhered to. We were about to contend with an enemy who gave no quarter. The fiat of Andries had gone forth; we were to travel on without pause until sunrise. Then we might sleep if the sun permitted.

At length the seemingly interminable night ended: "the phantom of false morning," which so often had mocked us, gave place to dawn—virginal and splendid. Then day came on rapid feet. Just as the sun cleared the rim of the earth the wagon halted, and at once the yokes fell from the necks of the tired oxen. Within a few minutes we lay fast asleep beneath a hastily-constructed sun-screen.

Scarcely more than an hour had elapsed before the heat awoke us and we sprang to our feet with hardly a trace of fatigue. The strong sunshine seemed to sting us to vigour; it was aether rather than air that we breathed. Around us lay infinite expanses, glowing and quivering,—radiating fervour against fervour into the moveless atmosphere. Before us and to our right and left the horizon was unbroken. Behind us could still be faintly traced the contour of the hilly country from which we had yesterday emerged.

The oxen, after feeding a little, wandered about—attempting from time to time to escape homeward. They dreaded this plunge into the waterless waste. They instinctively anticipated the heavy sufferings to which they were doomed. So far they were not painfully thirsty; cattle bred on the borders of the desert in their search for pasturage often go voluntarily waterless for forty-eight hours at a stretch. Even in summer they do not feel this much of an inconvenience. Late in the afternoon the team was driven up and once more inspanned. Again we pressed forward on our course.

The heat was still intense; we knew it would last until sundown. The primrose-tinted carpet of the desert seemed to have turned to flame. Before us some mocking genius of the sky painted mirage-pictures. Blue seas gemmed with verdant islands, rocky beaches from which sprang groves of lofty trees,—mountain ranges clothed with boskage and suggesting cool streams in their valleys—enticed us onward. Now and then the pictures grew distorted; occasionally they became inverted in the twinkling of an eye. Then the mountains stood poised upon their summits and the trees hung downward. Perhaps the operator of the magic lantern which projected these phantasms on the sky-screen was the vizier of the Thirst King—striving to lure the unwary to a terrible doom.

Although the heat was so intense, we were not badly distressed by it. The thrill of the unaccustomed exhilarated us; each breath we drew was as a draught of new wine. Interesting and unusual incidents befel. Ever and anon a troop of ostriches sped over the plains, their white plumes outstretched and thrilling. On the right, arising from the hollow of an undulation upwards of a mile away, could be seen a small thicket of "black sticks." Irregularly grouped and standing at various angles they shewed clear and distinct through the miraculously transparent air. "Gemsbokke," said Andries, laconically. The bodies of the oryx were out of sight; nothing was visible but their long and almost straight horns. Soon the earth-tremor betrayed us, and the thicket of "black sticks" became agitated. It broke up, scattered and reformed in smaller thickets. Then a herd of about fifty oryx swung at a gallop out of the hollow and sped up the wind, leaving a long trail of dust to mark its course.

Night fell again; again the star-curtain descended. At about ten o'clock we once more outspanned. There was not a breath of wind. The desert was vocal with unfamiliar sounds. The weird cries of the jackal were borne from afar across the plains; the clucking lizards put out their heads and conversed from burrow to burrow; the plaintive notes of the night-flying grouse fell from the sky like a rain of echoes. Under the protecting wing of darkness the solitude became populous and vocal with strange tongues.

We inspanned after an hour's rest. The longest and most wearying effort of our pilgrimage had now to be undertaken; our journey's end had to be reached before the yokes again were loosened. The night seemed endless; we were spent from the long travail. The yearning for sleep became acutely painful. We swayed and staggered as we followed the creaking wagon.

Dawn broke at length, but we were too weary, too undone to enjoy its loveliness. As the light grew we became aware of an abrupt eminence of granite on our left front; it arose, in the form of a steep cone, from a monstrous, agglomerated mass of copper-tinted, shapeless hummocks. This was Bantom Berg,—the "Belted Mountain,"—its red-cinctured bulk bathed in the first sunbeams, its feet entangled in the illimitable coils of the dune-tract. The latter at once seized and held the attention.

When day had fully dissipated the faint haze of morning we endeavoured to appraise the contours of this gross, amorphous entity,—for the concept that it was one and indivisible had gradually but irresistibly formed. It grew more and more enormous; more gross and inimical. Irregular and convoluted ridges arose from it here and there; it appeared to be absolutely bare of vegetation. In the centre was piled a humped, bulging mass; out of this Bantom Berg lifted its clean-cut cone of granite,—a soaring sphynx still waiting for the carver's chisel. Here and there columns of dust—slender beneath but widely dilating above at an enormous height, stalked slowly over the body of the prone monster, marking each the path of a miniature whirlwind. As we drew near, the face of the dune-tract once more became indefinite and complicated; for a time the eye could not follow nor appraise its details. But suddenly the thing explained itself; from the central mass, the prostrate carcase of the obscene creature, a number of league-long tentacles, consisting of sand-dunes, extended. These were thick at the base, but they tapered away to nothingness. Like a crouching spider or a half-huddled cuttle-fish the monstrosity sprawled,—its talon-tentacles seeming to gather in the plains—to infest them like a malignant cancer.

The character of the country we were traversing had changed; again the ground was hard beneath our feet; angular fragments of limestone were strewn over its surface. It was as though the dune-devil had collected and assimilated the surface sand so that its loathly limbs might develop. Inexpressibly sinister was this creature,—this mysterious, insatiable intruder from the desolate northern wastes. It seemed to be endowed with some low-graded form of rudimentary life; otherwise it was hard to account for the definite and arbitrary variations in the scheme of its southward advance. For the tentacles did not all extend in the same direction; occasionally one curved in its course and developed against the prevailing wind. The dune-monster was the slow-pacing steed of the Thirst King; it was his throne, his host and his strong city; it was the abhorrent body of which he was the resistless and implacable soul!

Our camping-place lay within the curve of one of the tentacles; it was expedient from the stand-point of the hunter to have the mounded sand between us and the plains—thus affording concealment. The sun was high when the yokes dropped once more. The unhappy oxen, now very thirsty, wandered about emitting low moans of distress. Their fundamental instincts told them that no water was near; their inherited faith in the wisdom and power of man had, however, given them the thought that relief might be provided. Suddenly, however, primordial instinct gained ascendency; their minds were made up. They paced, lowing, to the trail; then advanced along it at a trot. Soon the trot altered to a wild gallop. To-morrow, before noon, they would charge down on

10

Gamoep—and woe to man or beast obstructing their course. Red-eyed, and with blackened tongues extended from roaring, tortured throats, they would fling themselves into the pool and drink their fill. At Gamoep they would remain for four restful days; then they would be brought back to our camp by Piet Noona and his nephew.

So at length we were within the dominions of the Thirst King—our gauntlet thrown down at the gates of his wrath; we were almost within the grasp of his awful hand. The last link with the world inhabited by men snapped when the hapless oxen disappeared over the rim of the desert. Like a water-logged ship in a tideless sea—like a derelict among the Sargossa weeds,—the wagon stood in the solitude and silence, with the cloudless sky above and the sun-scorched earth beneath—with the dune-fiend watching us from his lair. It was almost an insult to the landscape—this wood-and-canvas construction of man, hauled jolting and groaning across the pathless desert by tamed and tortured beasts. It was a disfigurement on the face of Solitude,—an incorporate insult flung like a guage against the ramparts of one of Nature's most jealously guarded fortresses.

Under the shadow of the wagon-sail we slept throughout the day; the sun was down before we awoke. Once more night put on the garment of life. It was a desert-dweller who wrote that the heavens declared the glory of God; the first astrologer must have had his home in the wilderness. Over the desert the stars, unfolding a glory not revealed elsewhere, descend like a swarm of bees and seem to busy themselves with destiny.

Whispers of ghostly voices close at hand,—faint and far-off cries,—flutters of spectral wings—pulsed through the darkness. In the desert, the brighter the firmament at night, the more intensely darkness seems to brood over the earth,— the more insistent becomes the idea that one is surrounded by living beings, unhuman and unimaginable.

Hark! a sound of sinister import; involuntarily one sprang to grasp the rifle standing against the wagon-wheel. But an instant's reflection brought reassurance; it was but the booming of an ostrich far out on the plains that had conjured up scenes of other days,—when questing lions prowled around camp fires, now long since quenched. The most experienced ear can hardly distinguish the distant voice of a lion from that of an ostrich. Here, however, we might rest unscathed by beasts of prey; the only possible danger was from cobras and horned adders which, being unable to sustain the heat of the earth's surface by day, remain underground and emerge by night to practise their respective trades.

Sleep, sudden and imperative, would not be denied; we had the arrears of two wakeful nights to pay. Dune, desert and star,—past, present and future—what were they? Where were they? Whither was the awakening night-wind bearing us?

Chapter Three.

The Search for Meat—Death of the Oryx—The Flank of the Dune—
Outwitting a Jackal—Hendrick, My Guardian—Thirst—The Distant
Rain—Typhon—The Southern Simoom.

Daybreak found us sitting close to the candle-bush fire, for the air of morning
was chill. Soon the kettle boiled and coffee was prepared. Meat was badly
needed; we had eaten the last of the sand-grouse on the previous day, and a diet
of unrelieved rusks is apt to pall. So we decided that I was to take my rifle and,
accompanied by Hendrick, go forth in search of something to shoot.

Hendrick and I shaped our course along the western flank of the dune-tentacle
close to which we were camped, meaning to cross it near its point of emergence
from the main dune. On reaching a suitable spot we climbed to the top, a height
of some twenty feet vertically, and carefully scanned the plain on the eastern
side. The light was yet faint and, as we were facing the east, otherwise
unfavourable. While we lay prone a jackal shambled up the steep slope of loose
sand and met us, face to face. The creature regarded us with quaint
bewilderment for a second, and then scampered back with a yelp of dismay.

So far as we could ascertain the plain before us was empty of game. Gloom,
intensified by contrast with the developing pageant of morning, still lurked
among the shrubs and tussocks. In front, some six hundred yards away, lay
another dune-tentacle. This did not, however, extend in quite the same direction
as the one we occupied, its course being a few degrees more to the southward
for the greater length, while the extremity curved slightly back towards us. The
intervening space was soon crossed. Once more we clambered up through loose
sand that flowed at a touch; then we lay prone on the flat top, searching with
expectant eyes the new expanse revealed.

The light had now improved; a limitless plain opened to south and east.
Northward, the wind-scourged side of the main dune extended like a sea-worn
cliff. The faint, diaphanous suspicion of haze incidental to newborn day, which
lay film-wise over the yet-unawakened desert, did not interfere with our vision.

A twenty-foot elevation gives the eye an immense range. Game was now in
sight; five separate groups of ostriches could be located. These were miles
apart,—their units varying in number from five to twenty, or thereabouts. Away
in the dim distance southward some large animals were visible; they moved
slowly westward. These were almost certainly oryx. About six hundred yards
off, straight before us, was a small herd of springbuck; they were busily grazing,
moving to the right as they grazed. This circumstance, combined with the fact
that the oryx were moving in the same direction, indicated that out on the plains
there was an air-current from westward; consequently there was some likelihood
of the day being fairly cool.

The springbuck were too far away to fire at; probabilities would have been too
much in favour of a miss. On foot in the desert, missing one's shot meant that
one's chances of obtaining meat were practically at an end for the day. So there
was nothing for it but to wait. Perhaps a paauw (bustard) might feed up to within
range. We had seen many paauws on the wing the previous day.

What most surprised us was the number of jackals. Several of these sneaking marauders were visible, loping here and there. One approached the springbuck; a ram put down his head and charged straight at the intruder. The latter fled, yelping dolorously. The buck, his head still lowered, pursued, and gained easily upon the fugitive who, hard pressed, doubled over and over again on his devious course. At length the jackal took refuge in a burrow, and the buck trotted back to join his mates, who had apparently taken no notice of the incident.

Hendrick touched me slightly on the shoulder, and uttered a slow "s-s-t." I glanced to the left; my heart leaped almost to my throat. There, pacing towards us at a leisurely stroll, was a lordly oryx bull. He was about eight hundred yards off; evidently he had been lying down with his horns concealed behind one or other of the bushes that here and there studded the plain. Most likely he was a rogue; an old bull turned out of the herd on account of his bad temper,—or possibly a leader deposed by a rival. However that might have been, he represented meat—a commodity we were badly in need of. Ever and anon the oryx halted and gazed anxiously along the flank of the dune; then he resumed his advance, pacing steadily on a course which should have brought him to within about two hundred yards of our ambush.

Nearer and nearer the bull approached; he seemed to be suspicious, for his muzzle was held high and his large ears moved backward and forward. Probably our camp had tainted the air for miles in every direction. "Tshok-tshok" uttered a paauw which we now noticed for the first time. The bird was sauntering on a zig-zag course and occasionally pecking among the shrubs just beneath us. Its approach was from the right; thus it was advancing towards the oryx. The moment was a critical one; should the paauw have taken alarm and flown, the oryx would undoubtedly have galloped straight out towards the plains as fast as his strong legs could carry him. If, on the other hand, the paauw passed and remained unaware of our presence, the oryx would have inferred that the coast in our direction was clear, and accordingly have come unsuspiciously within easy range. So we lay as still as mummies, Hendrick and I,—almost afraid to breathe.

The crisis passed. The paauw was soon well beyond us, and the bull, accelerating his pace slightly, advanced to his doom. O! you of the swift feet, the tireless thews and the long, sharp horns that even the hungry lion dreaded,—you had run your last course, you had fought your last fight; the sands of your lordly life were running low!

The great oryx bull was now only about two hundred and fifty yards off. Something startled him; a whiff of tainted air stung his sensitive nostrils. He stood half-facing us, his right shoulder exposed. My rifle, a long Martini, had been trained on him for some seconds, awaiting a favourable opportunity. "Crack"—and the bull fell huddled on his left haunch. He sprang up, but floundered pitifully. Hendrick and I were now over the dune and running towards him. As we approached, his struggles ceased; he no longer attempted to escape. He was standing on three legs, for his right shoulder had been smashed and the limb dangled loosely.

13

The bull was an awe-inspiring sight. Every separate one of the wire-like hairs on his neck, shoulders and hump stood erect and quivering. His wide nostrils shewed blood-red in their depths; his eyes blazed with agony and wrath; he swayed his forty-inch-long horns menacingly from side to side, as though to test their poise.

The brave brute was evidently co-ordinating his maimed but still formidable strength for a charge at his enemy. "Schiet, Baas—anders kom hij" ("Shoot, Sir—or he will come") yelled Hendrick. I had the bull carefully covered, and as he swayed forward in the first impulse of attack, my bullet struck him in the middle of the neck and crashed through the vertebral column. Then the strong, tense form collapsed and sank impotently to earth.

He was a noble beast,—this creature whose life I had wasted. Why had I done it? Because I wanted meat; because I followed the law of my being in obeying the hunters' instinct,—almost the deepest and strongest in man. The answer was, of course, not quite a good one; I felt it could not be supported on ethical grounds. But conventional ethics belonged, after all, to an environment I no longer inhabited. Where I then lived and moved and had my being, the unmoral standards of primeval man prevailed.

A shout from the top of the dune. It was from Andries and the others who, on hearing the first shot, hurried over to see what my fortune had been. We returned in triumph to the wagon, carrying the liver of the slain oryx. This would be roasted on the embers for breakfast. Hendrick and his assistants would see to it that the rest of the meat, the head and the skin were removed and properly treated. Very soon the carcase had been dismembered and carried piecemeal to the camp. After the skin had been stretched out and spalked down to dry on the hot sand, we cut up and slightly salted the meat, preparatory to its being packed together and rolled in sacking. Next day it would be hung out on lines to dry into "bultong." The head was a beauty; the horns measured 41.5 inches. That night the jackals from far and near would pick up the scent and prowl, yonking and yowling, about the camp. The less cowardly among them would steal up— almost to our very hearth. Consequently we should have to avoid leaving unprotected anything capable of being chewed. The jackal is the Autolycus of the desert.

In the afternoon I explored the south-western flank of the main dune. So light was the sand that in parts I sank almost knee-deep. Jackals were to be seen everywhere; one wondered how such a number could manage to eke out a livelihood in so barren a locality. From one hollow,—a cup-shaped depression scooped out by some recent wind-eddy, seventeen of these animals emerged. They were too far away to fire at, for I had left my rifle in camp and brought a shotgun. There was no other sign of animal life.

Fold upon fold—utterly, unspeakably arid—the flank of the main dune sinuated away towards the north-west. On turning towards the north the abomination of desolation grew more abominable at every step, so I altered my course to the left and descended the steep side of the red-hot dust-heap. Soon I found myself on the edge of a plain lying between two dune-tentacles which were about a mile apart. In more or less the centre of this plain was a small patch of low scrub, and towards the latter a single jackal was loping. He was of the "silver" variety; consequently his pelt was of value. I felt I wanted that pelt. The only good jackal is a dead jackal. I had no qualms of conscience about taking this creature's life.

My slinking friend whose opulent coat of silver-striped fur I coveted, reached the little patch of scrub and crouched down in it. But the bushes were so low and sparse that I could distinctly see his erect, pointed ears. Now,—I meant to have some amusement out of that marauder, that prowling scoundrel who butchered young fawns and plundered the nests of birds. So I lit my pipe and strolled,—not towards the patch of scrub; that would have been far too obvious a thing to do,—but as though I meant to pass it by some distance to the right. I did pass it, but immediately afterwards inclined my course slightly to the left, proceeding in a curve. The curve became a spiral; I walked round and round the patch of scrub, gradually edging nearer.

To look towards the jackal would have been to give myself away absolutely. My game was to pretend to be unaware that such a thing as a jackal existed in Bushmanland. However, out of the tail of my left eye I could just see the pointed ears still erect; it was clear that the owner of those ears was following my movements with careful but perplexed attention. Was it possible that that villain, with all his cunning, could have really believed that I was taking just an ordinary stroll? The fact was,—he found himself face to face with a wholly unprecedented situation.

Of course I recognised that all my trouble might be for nothing; that the jackal perhaps was sitting at the side of a convenient burrow, ready to drop out of sight at my first suspicious gesture. But, on the other hand, were no burrow available, my cunning friend's moments were drawing to a tragic close,—his last springbuck fawn had been devoured, his last smashing of ostrich-eggs perpetrated.

I was now within sixty yards of the jackal; still there was no movement on his part,—except that of the pointed ears which followed the following eyes. The distance decreased as the spiral drew in; the Lachesis-web was being spun fine; Atropos stood ready with her shears. Fifty—forty yards—now he must be very uneasy indeed. There was evidently no burrow available; otherwise he would long since have disappeared into it. He had never seen anyone manoeuvre like this; how he wished he had bolted when I first altered my course. Thirty— twenty yards;—that was more than he could stand. He hurled himself forth— only to fall, riddled by a charge of buck-shot.

Hendrick came running across the flat, his face beaming with delight. There would be joy in the camp that night, for jackal-flesh is the Hottentots' favourite delicacy.

Try as I might, I never—in the course of my various Bushmanland trips—had been able to shake Hendrick off, for my friend Andries had issued strict injunctions that he was never to lose my spoor. So whenever I left camp, Hendrick made careful note of the direction I had taken and, after an interval, followed me. No notice was taken of the protests I made against this, as a rule, wholly unnecessary precaution, for Andries had a strong arm and a sjambok for use when his servants disobeyed him. Westward of Gamoep, Andries as a rule did what I told him to, but in the desert he was an autocrat, and a severe one. I believe that in Bushmanland he would have sjamboked me had there been no other way of enforcing his will.

Andries distrusted my desert craft, making no allowance for that "sense of direction" which strenuous wanderings of early years in waste places had developed in me. However, hunting in the desert was undoubtedly fraught with danger. Under certain atmospheric conditions, if one had suddenly to put forth exertion sufficient to induce perspiration, the pores refused to close, and moisture was drawn out of the system at such a rate that to drink presently or die was the alternative.

The Bushmanland desert has taken a heavy toll of thirst-victims. Close to Agenhuis I was shewn a little bush under which a strong young fellow—the son of a man I knew well,—laid himself down and perished miserably within a mile of his camp. The people at Agenhuis saw him coming on, walking slowly. He turned out of the track and sank under a bush; those who watched him thought he had paused to take a rest. Wondering why he delayed so long, his friends strolled over to where he lay. The man was dead. His tongue was blackened and shrunk; his lips and eyelids cracked and caked with clotted blood. This is only one of the many dismal instances of people perishing of thirst within short distances of their camps.

The day died gloriously. Far away to eastward a thunderstorm trailed down from the north, its bastions and buttresses snow-white or ebon-black—according as to whether the sunlight touched them or not. When the last level beams smote through the banked masses of vapour, a glory of rose, purple and gold transfigured the soaring turrets. That night the firmament was clearer than ever; the satellites of Jupiter could actually be seen with the naked eye. The eastern horizon was lit by Aurora-like lightning,—soft, lambent and incessant. Eastern Bushmanland must have been drenched. Even as I watched, the springbuck, scattered over the western desert, had no doubt read the signal aright and begun their hundred-mile flitting towards the regions blest with rain. Already the Trek-Boers at Namies and Naramoep would be busy pulling down their mat-houses and packing their wagons for the trek eastward. The barometer shewed a heavy fall; this indicated unsettled weather,—probably a strong wind from the north.

Mute, ominous and black loomed the dune-devil. Who and what was he, that unspeakable entity? Was he not Typhon, Lord of Evil and Autocrat of Desert Places—that monstrous deity who was cast forth from the councils of the Egyptian gods on account of his unspeakable iniquities? Yes,—it was Typhon and none other; he wandered south in search of a kingdom to usurp, and found it there. But the rain-god, whose throne is the distant Drakensberg, stretched forth his silver sword, the Gariep, and ham-strung the intruder. Otherwise the Kalihari might now be stretching forth a hand to grasp l'Agulhas, and all the African southland be a waste.

That embodied malignity, crouched and huddled beneath the sumptuous stars—what unspeakable outrage was his bestial and inchoate rudiment of a

16

mind devising? Perhaps that day he had sent a message bidding his hag-handmaid, the north wind, come and help him to destroy us, intruders. There was menace in the air. The temperature had hardly fallen,—as it almost invariably did at night.

At daybreak the atmosphere was tense, oppressive and phenomenally lucid. Often the desert dawn is followed by a faint semi-opacity; an opaline suggestion of vapourised moisture,—the diaphanous veil of evaporated dew. But on the previous night no dew had fallen. Heaven had withheld that gracious, healing touch with which it sometimes assuaged the scorch inflicted by the ruthless sun on the patient wilderness.

The plains lay hushed as though in anticipation of sinister happenings. Soon the east grew suddenly splendid; shafts of faint gold and delicate rose spread from the horizon half-way to the zenith. These were the wheel-spokes of the still-hidden chariot of the sun-god. The flanks of Typhon, the huddled shoulders between which his head was sunk, took on the hue of glowing bronze. The Belted Mountain shone like a bale-fire.

The sun arose; his first beams smote like the lash of a whip. In the twinkling of an eye the glamour of morning had shrunk and shrivelled,—fallen to the dust and left no more trace than would a broken bubble. The world was now a tortured plain on which the redoubled wrath of the sky was poured forth. Typhon seemed to stir in his sleep,—to expand and palpitate. The reason of his baleful and unbridled power was at hand. That day he would be omnipotent and unquestioned Lord of the Desert.

A faint, hushing breath, less felt than heard, touched us and passed on over the shuddering plain. Its course was from the north; it left increasing heat on its track. Another, not so faint, but definitely audible,—tangible as flame. It was indeed the breath of Typhon,—the suspiration of his awakening fury. A fringe as of erect russet hair plumed his hunched shoulders. Here and there immense tufts, like those of a waving, quivering mane, were hurled aloft; they fell back in the form of cataracts. Then—like the sudden smoke of a volcano, his loosened locks streamed forth on the tempest. Typhon was awake and had arisen in his blighting wrath.

His breath had not yet reached us, but it was very near. His voice was a penetrating, sibillant hiss, with a moaning undertone—the utterance of fury rendered inarticulate by its own intensity. Now the sand-spouts which had been flung upwards, rained on us in fine, almost impalpable dust, that scorched where it fell. It filled the air we strove to breathe; it blinded and baffled us as we vainly sought for shelter.

Then darkness settled down and the moaning undertone swelled to a roar. We crouched within the wagon, the tilt of which rocked and strained. The air we gaspingly breathed had a horrible, acrid taste.

Now and then a compensating current of air streamed back under the wing of the tempest that overwhelmed us, and afforded relief for a space. It was only during such intervals that we could venture to lift our eyes; it was then we saw that the red-maned tentacles around us were alive and writhing, and we knew that on the morrow their location and contours would be different from what they were that morning.

It was late in the afternoon when Typhon's rage subsided and we emerged from our ravaged wagon, which stood half-buried in sand. The tentacle near us had stretched out a feeler and grasped it to the axles. It took several hours of hard digging before we were able to liberate the wheels enough to admit of the wagon being drawn out and taken to a spot which was free from drifted sand.

Yes, the monster had moved; his shoulders were hunched at a different curve; his long flank had taken on strange bends and bulges. But he was once more prone after his terrific but impotent uprising. Typhon slept.

Chapter Four.

A Walk in the Darkness—Dreams of a Morning—The Scherm—The Slaying of the Ostrich.

Arched, sore, gritty and with overstrung nerves I sought my bed early, hoping that sleep would come soon and obliterate the effects of that day of turmoil. I meant to shoot an ostrich on the morrow. To make this practicable I should have to rise at 2 a.m., for it was essential that I should reach a locality at least six miles away before daybreak.

But the fiery breath,—the tawny, tossing mane of Typhon seemed still to envelop me; his moaning hiss yet filled my ears. I felt as if I had stood face to face with one of the Lords of Hell. The reek of Tophet was still in my nostrils. Midnight had passed before sleep came.

When Hendrick wakened me I felt as though I had hardly lost consciousness. It was the specified hour. Hendrick could no more read the face of a clock than he could decipher a logarithm, but he knew what it was we were going to attempt, and that if our adventure were to have any chance of success, we should set about it without delay.

Before waking me, Hendrick had brewed the coffee, so after hurriedly emptying a pannikin and adding a few rusks to the contents of my haversack, I seized a rifle and made a start. My course lay due south, my objective being the vicinity in which the troops of ostriches had been visible on the previous morning. It had been arranged that Hendrick was to start an hour later and make a wide détour to the right, for the purpose of stampeding any birds he could manage to get to the westward of. It was trusted that such birds might run towards the spot where I intended to lie concealed.

The sky was clear as a crystal lens, for the copious dew had caught all dust particles which were left suspended in the atmosphere after yesterday's outburst, and carried them back to earth. The waning moon had just arisen; fantastic shadows were cast by every shrub and tussock. The air was cool—almost cold; not a breath stirred. Every few yards I stumbled over irregular heaps of soft sand, varying in height, in size and in contour. These were fragments of the ravaged locks of Typhon—locks torn out in his fury of yesterday and flung far and wide over the desert.

18

How still it was; how void my environment of the details of ordinary experience. It was like a ramble through dreamland. The whirring wheels of Time seemed to have become dislocated; each as it were turning reversed on its axis—no two moving at the same speed. It seemed as though the mill of which sequence is a product had fallen out of gear, for yesterday joined hands with a day of twenty years old, while the intervening myriads of days flew forth into the void like chaff from a winnower.

Space seemed to have taken on additional dimensions,—the impossible to have become actual without an effort. Faces glimmered up through the mists that hung over the dimming pathway of the past—through the steam of long-shed tears—through the ghastly coffin-lid and the horrible six feet of clay. They smiled for an instant, and vanished. Winds that had slept for years arose laden with the laughter from lips whose warm red faded with dawns long overblown. Surely I must have strayed into some pallid Hades such as the ancients fabled of,—some zone where shadows only were real and real things appeared as shadows.

Mechanically I strode on, avoiding without conscious volition the shrubs and tussocks. As the moon ascended the shadows shortened and became less grotesque. Fancied resemblances to and suggestions of things outside my own experience, but of which my mind had formed concepts that had become familiar, switched thought on to other tracks; the pendulum swung from the subjective to the objective. Imagination built up the tiny, lithe, agile forms of that race we exterminated and whose barren territory we annexed, but neither occupied nor made use of. I could almost hear the sandalled, pattering feet of the aboriginal dwellers of these plains,—those kings of the waste whose sceptre was the poisoned dart. The Bushmen were in many respects a wonderful people. They obeyed no chief; they had no political organisation whatsoever; each family governed itself independently. Yet they had their fixed customs,—their general traditional code of proprieties. They had knowledge of the properties of plants which no others possessed; they had a highly-developed dramatic art. As limners they excelled, and a keen sense of humour is evinced in many of their paintings. Not alone was this sense of humour keen, but it must have been very much akin to our own.

How many hot human hearts have searched for a clue to the nature of that Power which energises as much through evil as through good,—which could foster the development of a numerous people under painful and inexorable laws until it harmonised with its rigorous environment,—that could implant in its units the capacity for love, heroism and faithfulness—and then ordain or sanction its obliteration,—an obliteration so absolute that, with the exception of one aged and senile pair, and a few delineations on sheltered rocks, of animals that shared its doom, this people has not left a trace behind. Literally, not a trace; hardly so much evidence that it ever existed as afforded in the case of an extinct sub-species of diatoms, the imprint of whose forms may be found on the fractured face of a chalk-cliff.

Musing thus, I suddenly became aware that day was at hand, for the pallid moonlight grew paler and the thrill of approaching dawn pulsated through the firmament. If all my trouble were not to be thrown away, I should at once select a spot suitable for my ambush. But first I had to look out for a certain shallow-rooted shrub of globular form which grew in patches here and there throughout the desert. A few such shrubs had to be pulled out of the ground and piled in the form of a low, circular fence enclosing a space about six feet in diameter. This is the "scherm" or screen so often used by those who hunt in the desert. Within it the hunter lies prone, fully concealed from any approaching quarry.

I was in luck, for I had reached an almost imperceptible rise; a long oval, the highest part of which was not more than thirty inches above the general level of the plain. But those inches were of incalculable value for my purpose, for they extended by miles the scope of my vision in every direction and, should game have been afoot, enabled me to prepare for the one and only shot. A single shot each day is the utmost that the hunter on foot in the desert ever expects.

In the vicinity of the rise shrubs were fairly plentiful, so I plucked out a sufficient number of suitable size and drew them carefully to the spot I had selected for my lair. This was just to westward of an unusually high shrub, a "taaibosch" which, after the sun should have arisen, would afford temporary shade for my head. But day came on apace; no time was to be lost.

Within a few minutes my scherm was complete, and I extended prone within it. After consideration I ventured to light my pipe. There was no wind; even had there been the ostrich has no sense of smell,—and on that day I was not looking for buck. Even had an oryx approached and sniffed at me, I would have let him go scathless. An ostrich, and a super-excellent one at that, was what I wanted. No breeding bird with plumes discoloured through contact with the sand, but a young, lusty, unmarried male with peerless adornment of foam-white plumes,—the crowning result of a long period of selection,—developed by unrestricted Nature for the all-wise end of making him comely in the eyes of the female of his species.

It was now day, although the sun was not yet visible. I was in my shirt-sleeves, having left my jacket at the camp. The faint wind of morning was chill, the dew-soaked ground dank and cold. I longed for the sun to rise, albeit well knowing that after it had risen my discomfort from heat would be intense, and that I would look back to the hour of the dew and the dawn with vain regret.

Cautiously and very slowly I lifted my head until my eyes could search the plain in the direction from which Hendrick was operating. But I hardly expected to see him yet. Void, cold, passionless and austere the still-sleeping desert stretched to the sky-line. The dominant note of its colour-scheme was creamy yellow, with but a hint of sage-green,—for the plumy shocks of the "toa" far outnumbered the sparsely-scattered shrubs. A glance at Bantom Berg and Typhon shewed them to be touched by the first sunbeams. The shoulder of the dune-monster shone as though a radiant hand were laid upon it. The hand stole tenderly down the side and flank, revealing unsuspected scars. It was as though the morning were caressing the loathly creature,—trying to heal with pitying touch his self-inflicted scars of yesterday. In the limitless expanse of desert Typhon and his granite prisoner stood isolated,—the only prominence, and the ungainly bulk of Typhon made manifest the immensity of the kingdom he had usurped and the illimitable extent, of the territory towards which his carking hands outstretched.

The sun was now up and the resulting warmth was a physical delight. But I could not avoid lugubrious anticipation of what all too soon was coming,—that fierce ardour which would cause the sand to grow red-hot and make my couch, then so comfortable, a bed of torment. Why should this anticipation have almost destroyed my physical pleasure? why should mind and body thus have been set at variance with each other as the sense of grateful warmth penetrated my shivering limbs? It is this kind of thing that places man at a disadvantage as compared with other animals, who live in the immediately existing time. No matter how fair the flowers or how rich the fruits of the present may be, a menacing hand stretches back from the future and touches these with blight. When the Apostle of the Gentiles wrote that he died daily, he merely cried out under the lash of that curse of foreknowledge which is at once man's glory and his doom. And the farther the eyes of man pierce into the future, the more terrible will be the things revealed.

A yelp; then many yelps,—faint, but clear as a tinkling bell. They came from the side opposite the one from which I expected the game to be driven. Cautiously I sank back, wormed myself round and looked over the edge of the scherm in the direction from which the sound came. A jackal, of course,—but why was he yelping? The reason was quickly apparent. About seven hundred yards away stood two ostrich hens. Running hither and thither, in hot pursuit of the jackal, was the cock bird. Autolycus was hard pressed; it was only by constant and cunning doubling and twisting that he was able to escape the sledgehammer kicks,—any one of which, had it got home, would have broken his back or ripped out his entrails. The chase trended in my direction; as the pursued and the pursuer approached I had an excellent view of it. At length the prowler reached his burrow and hurled himself incontinently in, his brush describing a frantic arc as he disappeared. The ostrich, fuming with disappointed wrath and flicking his wings alternately over his back, to work off his indignation, stalked with stately gait back to his wives.

Evidently this was a breeding trio, and the nest was not far from where the hens were standing. No doubt what happened was this: the birds arose from the nest for the purpose of allowing the eggs to cool. Then the jackal, who had made his burrow in the vicinity as soon as the nest had been established, attempted to play off his old, well known, but often effective trick. This consists in stealing up to the nest in an unguarded moment, pawing out one of the eggs to the top of the circular mound by which they are surrounded, and then butting it with his nose hard down oft the others. If the contents of an egg thus broken were fresh, the jackal would lap it up; if the chicken should already have been formed, so much the better for the thief.

These birds did not interest me that day; they and their nest formed a domestic menage which should not be interfered with,—except of course, by jackals and their confederates, the blackguardly white crows that carry small, heavy stones high into the air, and drop them on the eggs. An ostrich nursery in the desert requires much careful management and must be a source of constant anxiety.

21

I will not say that I had begun to regret my adventure; nevertheless the sunshine had waxed fiercely hot. My head was still within the small and decreasing patch of shadow cast by the taaibosch, but my back—and more especially my shoulders—suffered badly. I wished Hendrick would hurry. That game; was afoot was almost certain; otherwise he would long since have appeared. My trusty scout evidently had seen the advisability of making a détour wider than the one originally proposed. He was no doubt exercising every wile of his comprehensive veld-craft towards getting me a shot. His work was more arduous than mine; nevertheless I wished I could have changed places with him if only for a few minutes.

When I realised that my back was getting really overdone I turned over and exposed in turn each side, and eventually the front of my body, to the sun. Then I felt overdone all round. Moreover the vestige of shadow in which my head cowered—that cast by the sparse top of the taaibosch, through which the sunlight leaked freely—grew more and more scanty. Oh! I breathed, for a return of that blessed coolness of morning which my frame, softened by years of a semi-sedentary life, had been unable to sustain without discomfort. Oh! for the gentle, healing hand of the dew, which I so ungratefully contemned. If these desert plants can feel and think, how they must long for the night,—for the miracle of cool moisture which, perhaps, a beneficent planet distils in some grove-garden of the asteroids and seals up in the crystal vats of some celestial tavern known only to its sister spheres and the moon.

Surely there is some hostel of mercy in whose cool cellars the precious vintage lies hidden from the rapacity of the cruel sun,—held in readiness to be poured out from the etherial beakers of the firmament on the tortured tongues of the leaves and grass-blades, when the tyrant of the skies departs for a season.

My physical condition had become acutely serious on account of the increasing heat and the more nearly vertical vantage of the sun's arrows. The actual, immediate pain was bad enough,—but how about consequences. Saint Lawrence no doubt ascended to Paradise from his gridiron, but I should have to toil on foot over miles of desert after arising from mine. Even if I thereafter soaked myself in olive oil, days of blistered misery might have been in store for me. Oh! for a cloud or for Hendrick. If he only had arrived within sight I might have vacated my couch of anguish without forfeiting his respect or my own. The loss of expected sport became unimportant. Ostrich shooting in the desert from a scherm was far more than my fancy had painted it.

Hist! What was that? It was not a sound; hardly was it a tremor. It was rather a thrill not perceptible to any one sense; something apprehended by the nameless perceptions of the noumenon-area lying deep beneath the phenomena of sensation. I risked sunstroke by discarding my hat; then I slowly lifted my head until I could look over the edge of the scherm. At what I saw misery hid her face; mind once more assumed command of body.

The plain to the south-west was dotted with moving ostriches. Singly, in twos, in threes, in tens—they were speeding north-eastward over the desert; some on my right, some to the left. Ever and anon one or other of the groups halted and its members stood at gaze. The ostrich cannot keep on the move continuously for any length of time on a hot day. If forced to attempt doing so, death from heat-apoplexy would inevitably result. One troop, far in advance of all the others, seemed to be approaching me, but it swerved and passed to the left. It contained eleven birds, most of them young and immature; a few were full-grown hens and one was a very large cock bird. However, his plumes were sand-stained, so it is evident he had been dislodged from a nest.

Far and near there must have been nearly a hundred birds in sight. No doubt some favourite food was plentiful in the vicinity from which they had been stampeded; possibly a swarm of locusts might have there hatched out. Now the birds were beginning to scud past between me and the camp, as though following a trail known to them. But they were too far off to fire at. Could it be that after all I was not to have a shot.

Another troop swerved to a course calculated to bring them fairly close to the scherm; there were eight birds in it. They paused and stood at gaze for a short interval, about a mile away. Then they resumed their flight along a course which would, if they held it, bring them to within less than three hundred yards of me, on my right.

On they pressed with even, steady stride. Two were young but full-grown cocks with snow-white, sumptuous plumes. Cautiously I laid my rifle over the edge of the scherm and adjusted the sight to two hundred yards. The steel barrel scorched my fingers. Would the birds stand,—that was the question of importance. A running shot is always uncertain.

They halted when some two hundred and fifty yards away. Of the two gallant cocks one was manifestly superior; my bead was on him. I pulled the trigger; there was a tremendous report and the recoil nearly stunned me. My shot had missed. The birds sped away, at right angles to their original course. They became confused and ran hither and thither, for the near whiz of the bullet had alarmed them nearly as much as the distant detonation. But soon the bird I had fired at was speeding straight away from me. Within ten seconds I fired again, and he fell. The explanation of my having missed the first and easier shot is simple: I had foolishly allowed the cartridge to lie for a long time in the sun-heated chamber of the rifle; consequently the powder (one of the then new, smokeless varieties) had become too energetic. There was no violent recoil from the second shot.

I sprang from the scherm and ran to my quarry. There he lay, breast downward, his long neck bent and his head concealed under the black, bulky body. The wings were expanded, with the snowy plumes outspread, fanlike, on each side. The bird was stone dead, for the bullet struck the base of the spinal column and shattered it throughout the whole length. No swifter death could have been devised.

Carefully, one by one, I plucked out the lovely plumes. They were surely the fairest and purest ornaments ever devised by that influence which men, when the world was young, personified and worshipped as the Goddess of Love,—the noblest concrete expression of that principle which strives to draw sex relations to the higher planes of beauty. And here had I, a decadent human, typical of a

23

neuropathic age, destroyed this exquisite embodied achievement for the purpose of reversing Nature's plan. For I should transfer to the female, to my own woman-kind, adornments developed naturally on the male for the enhancement of his own proper beauty. The female ostrich, in her robe of tender, greyish brown, is attractive enough to her prospective mate without artificial aid. Were she to hang a wisp of human hair about her graceful, undulating neck, she would rightly be regarded as a freak.

Schopenhauer was right,—among human beings as among other animals the male is essentially more beautiful than the female; it is the sex-disturbance which confuses our canons. If it were otherwise women would not find it necessary to ransack mineral, vegetable and animal nature for the purpose of enhancing their attractiveness.

My plucking came to an end. The long, foamy whites,—the short, glossy blacks whose hue was deeper than that of the raven's wing,—were tied into bundles with twine from my compendious haversack. There lay the huddled, ruined, mangled body; there grinned the already dry and blackened blood-clot defacing the desert's visage. Rifled of its garment of harmonious and appropriate beauty, smitten and smashed into an object of grisly horror,—this piteous sacrifice to woman's callous vanity and the heartless cruelty of her mate seemed to make the wilderness as foul as the altar of Cain.

With an effort I passed from the stand-point of a somewhat inconsequent and inconsistent Jekyll to that of a primeval Hyde. From my flask, the contents of which had been carefully preserved intact up to the present, I poured out a libation to the manes of the departed ostrich. Might his freed spirit find refuge in some Elysian wilderness unvexed of prowlers who call chemistry and machinery to the aid of their own physical deficiencies, and slay because slaughter stimulates their debilitated pulses.

Far, far away to the south-west I saw faithful Hendrick approaching. I would not wait for him; he was too distant. My paramount need just then was shade— even if such could only be found under the tilt of a wagon where the thermometer probably stood at 112 Fahrenheit. Hendrick's needs were elementary; he would be delighted with the meat and the inferior black feathers which I had not thought it worth while to pluck. With the latter Hendrick and his kindred would adorn their disreputable hats. But their actions would be less opposed to Nature's plan than mine, for it was the men who would go sombrely gay, not their woman-kind.

The tramp back to camp was long and wearisome. Could it be that I strode along the same course whereon a few short hours ago I had paced hand in hand with gentle dreams? There,—on that dusty, gasping sun-scorched flat? Could it be that the stars and the soothing dew lay beyond that expanse of flaming sky, and that the laggard night, with healing on her dusky wings, would draw them down once more?

That day Danster was on his way from Gamoep with the horses. That afternoon Piet Noona and his imp-like nephew would hurry the oxen over the desert towards our camp; they should arrive the following night. On the next day

24

we intended to break camp and trek back westward. The return journey would not be so arduous for the cattle; we should have used up the greater part of the water, and the load would be correspondingly lighter.

The horses arrived soon after sundown,—old "Prince" with his deep chest, his powerful quarters, and his broad, shoeless, almost spatulate feet. The other horse, "Bucephalus," was a big, raw-boned black stallion which Andries had in training. Hendrick was, so far, the only one able to ride him.

Night once more—with the recurrent miracle of the dew-fall and the stars. Typhon slept. Of what was he dreaming? Of the far-off day when the overflowing measure of his infamy caused the decree of his banishment to be pronounced,—of the lands he ravaged and blighted on his southward course,—of his enemy, the rain-god, who smote him with the river-sword and thus crippled him for ever?

But man also must sleep—and on the morrow I had to journey to the Kanya-veld.

Chapter Five.

The Kanya—The Spell of the Desert—My Horse—The Terror of Noon—Execution of a Marauder.

Another glorious morning; the air was like cooled, sparkling wine. I knew, both by the taste and the direction of the wind, that the day would be as mild as it ever was in the desert at that season of the year. Through the faint dew-haze a hint of invitation—with a tender, enigmatic suggestion of a smile, shone out of the east. That was the day set apart for my journey to the Kanya-veld, the fringe of which lay about ten miles distant, beyond Typhon's eastern flank.

This is a region which lies solitary in the very heart of solitude. "Kanya," in the Hottentot tongue, means "round stone," and the Kanya-veld is thickly paved with such stones. They measure, as a rule, from four to eight inches in diameter, and they lie packed so closely that they nearly touch each other. They are buried to the extent of about two-thirds of their bulk in hard, red soil. Between them a scanty, hard-bitten, salamander-like vegetation strikes root. The Kanya-veld is hardly, if at all, higher than the rest of the desert. As to what the geological explanation of this strange phenomenon may be, I have no idea whatever.

No one knew the extent of the Kanya-veld, for that part of the desert had not then been surveyed, nor even roughly charted. Before reaching the main Kanya-tract one crossed narrow strips of the closely-packed spheres; these lay outside it, after the manner of reefs surrounding a coral island.

My journey of that day was to me the most important event of the excursion,—yet it had no definite object beyond the assuagement of that hunger for a realisation of the ultimate expression of solitude which sometimes gnaws at my soul. It was of what I was then to realise that I dreamt through night hours spent alone on a certain rocky hillside, when the east wind, with the scent of the desert on its wings and the music of the waste in its lightest whisper, streamed between me and the stars. But why try to explain the inexplicable? You who have not felt a like longing would never understand; you who have, will know without a word.

Prince stood ready girthed. Swartland—renamed "Bucephalus," the black stallion with the big head and the vicious, white-rimmed eye—was recalcitrant and resented the approach of Hendrick with the saddle. But I had decided to ride on; Hendrick was not to follow until the afternoon. I threatened that faithful follower with grievous penalties if so much as a silhouette of himself and his ugly steed shewed on my sky-line until after the sun had passed the zenith.

For we meant to be alone that day, Prince and I; to feel that we had got close enough to the heart of Solitude to hear its beats,—to try and capture in our ears, dulled by so-called civilisation, some syllables of that lore with which the desert's murmuring undertone is so rich, but which only the great of soul can fully understand. The cast of the desert's message is epic rather than lyrical. The cloud-mantled mountain and the green valley,—the forest, the stream and the foaming sea teach the poet his sweeter songs. But it is the Prophet of God, the law-giver and the warrior who listen for and learn their stern messages from the tongues of the arid wilderness.

The difference between the desert and the fertile tract is that between the ascetic and the full-fed man. The desert appeals to the intellect; the verdant, rain-nurtured valley to the emotions. The variance is as that between percipience and sensation. The stimulation with which a healthy organism responds to rigorous conditions expresses itself in an increased efficiency that is usually invincible. Thus it is that from the physically unfruitful desert all really great ideas have sprung. The wilderness has ever been the rich storehouse of spiritual things. Man gains corporeal, moral and intellectual power in the arid waste, and loses them in the land of corn and wine. Dearth is the parent and the tutor of thought, the desert is the harvest-field of wisdom. Solitude is the fruitful mother of noble resolve,—the kind nurse of the spirit.

THE OSTRICH AT HOME

I wished my horse had another, a more suitable name. "Prince" smacked of the stable—the brougham. He should have been called by some term expressive of steadfast endurance, of faithfulness,—of excellent skill as a pursuer of the oryx.

That elderly bay gelding with the spatulate feet was an ideal desert mount. It was in the course of a long chase after oryx that one appreciated him to the full. I had more than once ridden him at a gallop for ten miles without a check; then, after a roll in the sand, he was apparently as fresh as ever.

One of the dangers of a desert chase lay in the mouse-city, in which on getting entangled an ordinary horse was apt to check so suddenly in his course that he rolled head-over-heels and crushed his rider. But Prince had quite an original method of meeting the difficulty: he spread his legs out in some extraordinary way, sank down until his belly almost touched the ground, and floundered through. The strange thing was that he did not seem to break his stride. There was no jerk; the rider was in no way incommoded. I would have given a great deal for a side view of the performance; it must have resembled somewhat the progress of an heraldic griffin rampaging horizontally instead of vertically.

Where the surface was suitable, neither too hard nor too soft, we cantered slowly along,—careless as the wind that gently agitated the shocks of "toa." Game was at times in sight, but very far off. Three hartebeest sped away over the sky-line, their forms looming immense and grotesque just as the mirage seized them. I wondered what they looked like when thrown on the sky-screen and seen from a distance of fifty to a hundred miles. Oryx spoor, but not very fresh, abounded.

There were no ostriches visible. Those that on the previous day stampeded eastward had no doubt gone back during the night to the locality in which Hendrick had found them. A few springbuck were occasionally to be seen, but they were exceedingly wild. One would have had to manoeuvre to get within a thousand yards of them. Now and then a paauw flew up,—a forerunner of that immense migration which would take place a few weeks later. Then the whole paauw-population of the Kalihari would cross the Orange River and move over the plains by an oblique route towards the coast. They would return over the same course after they had nested and hatched out their young.

I had brought my rifle,—more from force of habit than anything else, for I was not anxious to shoot. I was content to gaze on the enthralling, impassive face with which the world there defied the arrogant sun; to admire that quality in it which I most lacked,—its steadfastness. I wanted to breathe the desert's breath, to drink of its life,—to do it homage and to love it—not for any fleeting beauty, but because my unsteadfast soul found it loveable and strong.

I had been on foot for some time. Prince, with the reins fastened short about his neck to prevent them trailing, followed like a faithful dog. Should I pause for what he considered too long an interval, he pushed me gently forward with his nose. He, too, wanted to explore—to wander on listlessly whither the spirit of solitude beckoned.

At length we reached the first strip of Kanya. It was hardly six feet wide,—that even, regular pavement of ironstone spheres laid down by the hand of Nature in furtherance of some aeon-old phase of world-development. Were those spheres forged in some volcano-furnace or turned in the lathe of the rolling waves in days when the temples of Atlantis gleamed white over the ocean that is its tomb and that bears its name? Were they slowly ground in the mill-vortex of some mighty river that bore away the drainage of a boundless humid tract, where now a rain-cloud is almost as rare as a comet?

Straight ahead, a little more than a mile away, the continuous Kanya-veld shewed like a darker wrinkle on the desert's brown face, for we were now out of the region of "toa." The stony strips grew wider as I advanced, and the intervening spaces narrower and narrower until they disappeared altogether.

Here Prince and I parted company for a while; I dared not risk the possibility of injury to those faithful feet that had carried me so swiftly and so far. Even proceeding at a walking pace in the Kanya, unless every step were carefully picked, involved a risk of sprain to ankle or fetlock. So I removed the saddle and tied my companion to a bush—not because I feared his straying, but for the reason that it was otherwise impossible to prevent his following me.

It was far hotter there among the Kanya than outside, for the dark-hued stones absorbed heat and radiated it fiercely. The desert's visage had taken on a sinister, forbidding expression; almost as though it resented intrusion—as though it had surrounded some shrine of secret horror with flame-hot, laming obstacles.

The only vegetation consisted of a few low, gnarled, bitter-looking shrubs. What an apprenticeship to inimical conditions these eremites of the vegetable world must have undergone to enable them to save their scanty leaves alive,— rooted, as they were, in a pinch of brick-like soil lying in narrow spaces between glowing spheres of stone, and lacking rain, as they did, for periods of years at a stretch. Their strength must have been as much greater than that of the oak as the oak's is greater than that of a willow sapling. Did these shrubs ever flower, I wondered. Perhaps, once in a thousand years, a miracle was wrought on them as it was on Aaron's rod. Only one could I identify—even so far as the genus went. It was a kind of Rhus; the dark-green, reticulated, trifid leaf—naked and deeply veined above and covered with down beneath,—was quite typical.

For what unspeakable cosmic sin was that titanic and seemingly eternal punishment inflicted,—that withdrawal of living water from a region built up and, no doubt, filled with abounding organic fecundity by the craft of its strong, creative hand? Did multitudes of those fearsome monsters of the prehistoric sea, which there swayed beneath the moon, gasp out their lives on that sun-blasted tract when the great cataclysm befel? Did a livid network of their colossal bones lie there for unthinkable ages until the slow attrition of wind and changing temperature transmuted them into that dust which vainly tried to scale the immutable heavens in the car of the sand-spout? Did the unanealed spirits of those long-dead creatures still people that haunted solitude which made day more terrifying than midnight? Were the landscapes of the mirage simulacra of those bounding an inland sea in which the dragon and the kraken lived and multiplied? Was the thrilling fear, which read menace in my own shadow, akin to that "terror of noon" which gripped the heartstrings of the shepherd of Mount-Ida,—when he knew, by the rustling of the brake that Pan was near?

28

I hastened away—back to where the desert wore a friendlier face,—to where old Prince was executing a kind of solemn dance before the "taaibosch" to which he was tethered,—lifting his feet constantly, one at a time, in a vain attempt to cool them. He welcomed me with a whinny of relief. Perhaps the spirits of the Kanya had been filling him, too, with indefinable dread. So the saddle was replaced, and I resumed my pilgrimage on foot, the old horse pacing stolidly after me.

We trended southward, for I wanted to get away from the Kanya; I began to hate it—almost as I hated Typhon. Yet I should not have hated either, for if it had not been for these two, the oryx, one of the desert's noblest denizens,—the aristocrat of its depleted mammal population—would long since have been exterminated. The Kanya is to the oryx a strong city of refuge from pursuit, and he draws his scanty but sufficient supply of moisture from the dunes coiled about Typhon's flanks. This seeming paradox is explained by the circumstance that a certain plant, the root of which somewhat resembles an exaggerated turnip and is heavily charged with moisture, grows in the dune-veld. This root the oryx scents out, and digs from out the sand with his strong, sharp, heavy hoofs.

The Kanya stones, which stop a galloping horse as effectively as would a barbed wire fence, are no obstacle to the oryx, for the divisions of his hoof expand widely and are connected by a strong membrane of muscle. They stretch apart when he treads on a stone, the membrane lying over the latter like a supporting spring. Yet, strangely enough, I once saw an oryx break its leg in passing over a narrow strip of Kanya. This occurred many miles from where I was that day; on the southern fringe of the Kanya-tract, in fact.

It happened in this wise. One morning Hendrick and I rode ahead of the wagon. Five oryx emerged from a depression and stood at gaze about six hundred yards away. I fired at the largest bull; he lurched half-way round, sinking partly on his haunches. But he at once sprang up and fled like the wind, completely distancing the other four. I followed, putting old Prince on his mettle from the start, for the Kanya was only about five miles away, and the wounded oryx was making straight for it.

The speed of the wounded animal slackened; not to any great extent, but enough to permit of the others slowly overtaking and then drawing ahead of him. When he reached the edge of the Kanya-tract I was about to give up the pursuit in despair, when the animal swayed in a peculiar way and then stood still, so I rode up and finished him. Then I found that the bone of his left fetlock had been freshly broken. My first bullet had, without touching the bone, passed through his right hind leg just where the great muscles of the haunch harden and thin down into sinew. The stroke of the heavy, leaden missile must have caused a severe mechanical shock. This, under stress of the gallop, evidently translated itself into stiffness, which occasioned leaning with undue heaviness on the sound leg. The oryx was crossing a strip of Kanya not more than twelve feet wide when the accident happened. Probably no similar occurrence has ever been witnessed by man.

My guardian-centaur, Hendrick-cum-Bucephalus, appeared on the north-western horizon. Yes,—it was time to turn back, for the sun had long since passed the zenith. Hendrick, as usual, looked supercilious when he found I had shot nothing. It would have been useless to have attempted to explain that Prince and I had come out that day only to talk secrets with the desert. Hendrick was too little removed from the natural man to be capable of understanding such a thing. He was an interesting creature, this Hendrick. A dash of Bushman blood in his veins had made him taciturn; the pure-bred Hottentot is almost invariably loquacious. But I found Hendrick an ideal companion. He, too,—without being aware of it, loved the desert for its own sake. But he delighted in seeing me make a good shot, and was almost pathetically puzzled on the occasions when I refrained from slaughter.

Hendrick did not on that day find it necessary to follow my sinuous spoor, but came straight towards where he knew I most probably would be. On his way he found an ostrich nest, with the inevitable jackal in its vicinity. He had chased the marauder away, but the parent birds fled too,—and in all probability Autolycus had, even before Hendrick found me, returned to the nest with nefarious intent. There was decidedly danger, for the birds, having fled after being disturbed, would not return before night. Well,—I determined to call on that jackal and, if possible, add him to the category of the righteous of his species.

We soon found the nest. Yes, as I expected, the robber had been at work. He must, in fact, have retired and concealed himself when he saw us approaching, for the evidences of his crime were quite fresh. No doubt he was peering at us from some cover close at hand while we were examining the results of his turpitude. Two eggs had been broken; their freshly-spilt contents were soaking into the sand.

We circled round, seeking for Autolycus' spoor. How I wished I had brought a shotgun instead of a rifle. Ha! there was the thief; he sprang from the shadow of a large tussock and ran diagonally away, his brush pointed contemptuously straight at us. What was his objective? I saw it—a heap of ejected sand about two hundred yards off, which he was heading straight for, evidently masked his burrow. I sat down, adjusted the sight of my rifle and drew the bead on the heap of sand.

When he reached the threshold of his refuge the jackal did exactly what a long experience of the habits of his obnoxious tribe had led me to expect,—that is to say he sank his hindquarters into the burrow and then turned to look back, as though in derision,—his head, chest and forelegs being exposed. Crack,—and he fell back and disappeared. But I knew well enough that the bullet had fetched him; I heard its "klop" distinctly.

Hendrick hurried to the jackal's burrow; I returned to the nest. The broken shells had to be removed and the spilt yolks sanded over; otherwise the birds would most probably have abandoned the clutch. There were three and twenty undamaged eggs remaining. Having put things as straight as possible, I rejoined Hendrick.

The jackal had disappeared into his burrow, but a big gout of blood just inside the entrance told an unambiguous tale. Hendrick wormed his way into the strait and narrow cavern as far as he thought he safely could; he emerged empty-handed, but with traces of blood on his clothing. However, Hendrick was not the Hottentot to forego a feast of jackal-flesh without a further effort, so he uncoiled a reim from the head-stall of Bucephalus, tied one end of it round his feet and gave me the other to hold; then he re-entered the dark portal and passed out of sight. Just afterwards I heard, as though from the bowels of the earth, a muffled shout. I hauled strenuously at the reim and Hendrick emerged, the dead jackal in his arms. In that cobra-haunted country I would not have attempted Hendrick's feat for a jackal-skinful of gold.

After this useful piece of police-work we rode back to camp at an easy pace. Bucephalus always grew cantankerous at the smell of blood, so the mortal remnants of Autolycus had to be tied behind my saddle,—a circumstance which occasioned a good deal of chaff on the part of Andries.

That night I spread out my large-scale map of South Africa on boards which I had brought for the purpose. It was my wont to fill in roughly any physical data which I was able to determine. The air was so still that the flame of a lit match hardly flickered. The vicinity of the wagon was as bright as day, for we had built an enormous fire. The flame of the candle-bush shone as clear as the electric arc, and arose in a tall pyramid. Our shooting was at an end, so we did not mind our presence being advertised throughout the desert. The oxen had returned from Gamoep. All preparations for a start before dawn on the morrow had been made.

After finishing my amateur map-making, I roughly measured with a pair of compasses the distance we had travelled from the vicinity of the Copper Mines. Thus I found that if we were to travel only four times as far, altering our course a little to the northward, we would reach Johannesburg. A change, indeed. How great would have been the contrast between Bushmanland, the abode of immemorial silence and solitude, and what was probably the most intensely active (in a mechanical sense) environment on earth. And yet, but a few short years before, when I first crossed it, the Rand lay as lonely as Bantom Berg. But now I could almost hear the ten-thousand-fold thudding of the stamps,—the thunderous explosions vexing the bowels of the earth—the din of the strenuous, diversified throng in the streets.

They say that men soon wear themselves out in the city of gold and sin; that the gravestones there are mostly those of the young. What is to be the effect of this burning fever-spot on our body-politic, of this—to change the metaphor— roaring maelstrom-mill into the hopper of which so large a proportion of the youth of our country is flung?

But in the nights that are coming,—when the rock-python pursues the coney along the shattered pediments of the "Corner House," the unchanging desert will lie, still void under the abiding scrutiny of the stars. Bushmanland can never alter.

The fire dimmed and died. One by one my companions sank into slumber. The horses were resting,—except unquiet Bucephalus, who stamped and whinnied at intervals. The oxen lay tethered to their yokes. Ever and anon one of them uttered the deep, pathetic bovine sigh,—that suspiration which seems to express perplexed resignation to the selfish dominance of man,—to that hopeless slavery which is the doom of the once-lordly bovine race.

I seized my kaross and climbed the steep side of the nearest dune-tentacle. Then I laboured along its soft, sinuous surface towards the gross, inert body of Typhon, until far beyond the reach of camp-sounds. In the yielding sand I made a lair. In this I laid me down—apparently the only waking thing in Bushmanland, for most utter silence reigned. Probably the soaring flames of our camp fire had frightened away even the jackals and the night-jars from a wide surrounding area. The stars seemed to sink earthward; so brightly did they glow in the vault of liquid purple that the face of the desert was masked in impenetrable gloom. That night the lips of the wilderness had no message audible to human sense.

Typhon slept—coiled about the feet of his granite prisoner, whose bulk loomed menacingly against the wheeling galaxies. Did he, the belted captive, sleep, or did he, haply, share vigil with the one solitary, futile human soul which, maimed from the stress of days and deeds, claimed with him brotherhood through pain and unrest. But slumber seemed to brood over the desert like a dove and a far-off voice to whisper across the shrouded plain: "Warte, nur— balde Ruhest du auch."

Chapter Six.

Homeward Bound—Faces around the Fire—The Bushmen—Piet Noona and the Snake—The Love of the Desert—My Prehistoric Uncle and Aunt—Scruples—The Hunter's Instinct.

The ocean-plain to the south of Typhon and the camp we had broken up, is probably the loneliest among the less frequented parts of Bushmanland. No Trek Boer ever ventures there with his stock; the hunter pauses on its undefined margin—well knowing that should he pursue the disappearing herd of oryx much farther, he and his horse would inevitably perish of thirst. For even on the rare occasions when rain falls on this tract no water is conserved on its surface. Those sand-choked, saucer-shaped depressions of the exposed bedrock found in other parts of the desert, in which rain-water sometimes lodges, do not there exist.

The only people who ever visited the area in which we sojourned were half-breed hunters. These had developed abnormal thirst-resisting powers. They usually occupied a tract some hundred miles farther south, and were incorrigible poachers of ostriches. By means of a flying squadron of boys mounted on tough ponies, these half-breeds used to round up herds, comprising birds of all ages, and mercilessly slaughter them all on the edge of the Kanya-tract.

We outspanned after a trek of about three hours. That night we intended to take things easy,—at least I meant to try and persuade Andries to consent to our so doing. The wagon was lightly laden, owing to our having consumed most of the water,—the heat had not been excessive since the oxen started from Gamoep; therefore they were not over-thirsty. In fairly cool weather cattle bred on the borders of the desert often voluntarily refrain from drinking water for several days at a time. We were homeward bound after a prosperous voyage. Supper was being got ready; Andries was busy preparing gemsbok soup, in which to soak our rusks. The candle-bush fire flared aloft. Our pipes were alight and the peace of the desert filled us with content.

Hendrick and Danster had skinned the second jackal which, in anticipation of the arrival of Piet Noona and his nephew with the cattle, I had insisted should be reserved for that night's supper,—for on the night previous we had trekked without a halt. The flesh of Autolycus was soon roasting on the embers; all our Hottentots were smacking their lips in anticipation of a feast.

I formally presented both jackal skins to Piet Noona's nephew,—but under an undertaking that they were not to be sold or otherwise alienated. The skin of the first jackal was too thoroughly riddled with buck-shot to be of much use to me; that of the second was badly torn by the bullet. They were to be brayed, mended, and donned by the recipient with as little delay as possible.

This gift might have been described as an offering on the altar of decency. I was not inclined to prudery, but Piet Noona's nephew was beginning to grow up, and his sumptuary condition was shocking. In fact his only available garment was a tattered fragment of sheepskin,—a fragment so scanty that it would have barely sufficed to cover the opening of a porcupine's burrow. Even then it could not have been guaranteed to keep out the draught. The jackal skins were not large, but compared with the sheepskin fragment they would have been as an overcoat to a child's pinafore. I explained how they were to be worn: one in front and one in the rear. The coverings of the hind paws were to be joined, skin to skin, in such a way that the combined result would hang from the wearer's shoulders, and the brushes were to be wound about his neck when the weather was chilly. Piet Noona's nephew would thus be reasonably protected, fore and aft, both from Mrs Grundy and the weather. Crowned with a chaplet of Ghanna leaves and with his knob-kerrie for thyrsus, he might have easily passed for a youthful but disreputable Dionysus.

As we drew out towards the borders of the desert the fingers of silence seemed to press less heavily on our lips. Supper over, we laid ourselves on the soft sand and conversed. But at first our conversation was low-toned and very serious. The imminence of infinity abashed us; it was as though earth and air were full of ears bent to catch every word we uttered. I do not think anyone,—even the most feather-brained, could be garrulous in the desert.

The flames lit up the surrounding faces,—the ruddy, rugged countenance of Andries, with its blue, laughing eyes and cropped beard streaked with grey. The visage of Piet Noona was like that of an old baboon; his nephew's resembled that of a young monkey. Danster's physiognomy indicated a mixture of various strains; the result was quite insignificant.

The Mongolian features of Hendrick were distinctive and very interesting. What was it that his appearance suggested; not exactly the Chinaman, for his expression was not at all impassive; one could always read his mood by it. His eyes were slightly oblique, his cheekbones high, his head was as round as a Kanya stone. With remarkable muscular development of the chest and shoulders, heavily hipped and very slightly bandy-legged,—for long I was puzzled to discover what is was that Hendrick reminded me of. He loved a horse and rode like a Centaur—or the man-part thereof. Then I knew: it was a Hun that I was seeking for,—one of the locusts of that Asiatic horde which swept over Europe from the north-eastern steppes. I think that Attila, the Eraser of Nations, who swayed the world from his saddle-throne, must have looked somewhat like my scout. The most plausible theory as to the origin of the Hottentot race is that its progenitors migrated hither from Asia. Even van Riebeek noticed the resemblance between the aborigines of the Cape and the Chinese. Yes, I was almost certain that Hendrick was a Hun,—or rather that the tribe he was mainly descended from and the Huns were twigs from the same bough of the great human tree.

Hendrick, to be appreciated, should have been seen on the back of an unrestrained or a vicious horse; it was then that he became a personality. He rode as gracefully bare-back as with a saddle. I could picture him galloping away from some sacked and smoking town—not on raw-boned Bucephalus, but on some thickset, shaggy, steppe-bred mount. Hanging limply across his tense, gripping thighs was a milk-white, gently-nurtured Ildico maiden. Her wide blue eyes were stony with horror,—her golden hair dabbled in the sweat of the horse's heaving flank. She was bound and pinioned with shreds torn from her robe of lawn. The other Huns were loaded with sacks of church plate, with weapons and with merchandise. But Hendrick looked on the face of this maiden, the daughter of what, but a few short hours before, had been a proud and noble house,—and desired her alone. But I think and hope she died of terror before the bivouac was reached. Hendrick was a tame, kindly, obedient hunting-scout, but I am sure that the fierce, conquering Hun lay sleeping within him.

There is not a watering place in the Bushmanland desert which has not some tragic story connected with it,—some reminiscence of a lonely thirst-death, some tale having for its motif the shedding of blood—usually by treachery. But death, accidental or designed, was always the theme. Not many miles from where we were camped that night one of the earlier Wesleyan missionaries travelling from Warmbad to the half-breed settlement on the Kamiesbergen had been shot to death with poisoned arrows. This happened early in the nineteenth century. The murderer was executed some time afterwards at Silverfontein.

The first white man who crossed this tract did a venturesome thing. For although at that time the Bushmen had already been considerably thinned out by the Hottentots and half-breeds, many of them still lurked in the less accessible parts. From time to time they emerged, singly or in small parties, and wreaked a wild and often quite inconsequent revenge.

Their mode of attacking travellers was to steal up at night among the tussocks and discharge a flight of poisoned arrows at point-blank range, among those surrounding the camp fire. They would then immediately decamp and scatter in the darkness. Hours afterwards they might repeat the attack. If the travellers were deep in the desert the repetition would perhaps be delayed until the following night, for the Bushmen took no avoidable risks. Usually the oxen or horses forming the span would also be slain. One can imagine the plight of a party of travellers under such circumstances: half of them dead or dying in agony, the survivors cowering in a wagon as hopelessly tethered to a lonely spot in a trackless waste as a wrecked ship is chained to the reef that gores her side. They would have been ringed round with drought and famine; close prisoners in a solitude only mitigated by the unseen presence of implacable foes, the stroke of whose dart was as silent and deadly as that of the snake.

Yet these Bushmen had sufficient justification for all the terrible reprisals they perpetrated. They were the original dwellers of the soil; the Hottentots came, dispossessed them of their best water-places and slaughtered them without mercy. When they migrated eastward they met the Kaffirs, who proved a more formidable and quite as pitiless a foe. In the storming of the Bushmen's strongholds their women and children were speared or flung into the flames. They retired to the most remote wastes,—to the sheer, black-chasmed fastnesses of the Malutis, where snow lies thick for months at a time,—to torrid, waterless deserts. But in every retreat, no matter how remote, their foes sought them out. They invariably made a desperate resistance, and sold their lives dearly.

But the duel was between ferocity organised and ferocity deranged, so the former was bound to prevail. It was a struggle of the clan against a number of units which had no permanent cohesion; whose combinations were fitful and occasional. There is no god but strength visible on the checker-board of history. When the mighty is put down from his seat it is not the humble and meek who is exalted, but one whose strength, being of a more subtle order, is perhaps not at first recognised as such—one whose cloak of humility may cover armour of proved temper. The strength of the Bushmen, perfected through long ages of experience, was all-potent against his one-time only adversary, the animal. But when used against man, the intruder who had fought for his existence with other men and learnt in the process the utility of combination, it failed. The Bushman contended under one tremendous disability: he had no tribal organisation,—the family was the independent unit.

Piet Noona's nephew, having had the duty of collecting fuel assigned to him, carried a considerable store of bushes to the vicinity of the fire and there heaped them together. With the exception of the "toa," most of the vegetation of the desert is globular in form, and, being usually rooted in more or less soft sand, is easily pulled out. Andries reached over and seized a bush-globe; one that was rather denser and larger than usual. This he flung on the fire. Out of it glided, hissing, a snake—a horned adder. The reptile was quickly despatched. But upon seeing it Piet Noona sprang into the air to a height of about four feet; then he fled away into the darkness, bounding sideways as he ran and shrieking. He had gone quite mad for the time being. This always happened when he found himself in close proximity to a snake, and the madness invariably manifested itself in the same way. Years ago Piet had been bitten by a puff adder and narrowly escaped with his life. Ever since the sight of a snake at close quarters has incontinently thrown his brain out of gear. How far occasional bouts of brandy-drinking at the Copper Mines has been responsible for this peculiarity, I cannot say.

Some months previously I had played—to a great extent unwittingly—a cruel trick on him. I had heard of Piet's being afraid of snakes, but had no idea that his dread of them was so intense. One day when he was saddling Prince I laid a recently-killed snake across the saddle. The creature was practically dead, but was still squirming slightly—as snakes are apt to do for a considerable time after they have been rendered harmless, no matter how badly they may have been mangled.

Piet's head, as he tightened the girth, was under the uplifted saddle-flap. When he dropped the latter and found the snake close to his face he sprang into the air and fled, bounding sideways and every now and then striking his thigh diagonally with the palm of his right hand. It was a most peculiar and uncanny manifestation. I did not see Piet for three days afterwards. Then he emerged from the veld, red-eyed and starving, but once more in his (comparatively) right mind. That night, as his cries grew fainter in the distance, we concluded that we should see no more of him during the trip.

Once more our caravan was silently moving over the trackless waste. The desert was now in one of her moods of tenderness,—the air full of soft and subtle scent that was sweeter than myrrh—more grateful than wafts from a garden of spices. A feeling of sadness gripped my heartstrings; I was leaving the mistress I loved—the mistress beneath whose stern, arid, monotonous day-mask I could discern the fair symmetry, the soft and delicately-tinted curves of perfect and eternal youth. How often had I breathlessly watched those features quicken and grow mobile as the defacing sun departed. It was then that the breath of her mouth sought mine; then that her eyes shone softly as the evening star. But it was at full night, when the great dome above us was unvexed by the least trace of day, that the desert's inhabiting soul came forth and transfigured the littleness of my cribbed and cabined spirit.

Sometimes for a season she smiled as though she relented, but the smile was not for me. At dawn, when Zephyr and Aurora couched at the hem of her robe, she let me lean against the softness of her bosom. At night she lulled me to sleep and crooned into my ear dream-songs that were great and strong with wisdom gleaned from the most ancient seasons. But when day returned she flung me to the lions of the sun. Should they have mangled me to death the mistress of my worship would not have cared. She was too strong to feel compassion, too lofty to be moved by grief or touched by any regret. My beloved was not mine, tho' I was wholly hers, and the lilies at her breast were petalled with consuming flame. "Who is she that looketh forth as the morning, fair as the moon, clear as the sun, terrible as an army with banners?" It was the desert.

Spinoza's aphorism:—"Those who love God truly must not expect that God will love them in return," roots deep in human experience. The loftiest love is that which gets not nor expects requital. I used to believe that this desert I love hated me. But I thought so no longer. It was not hate nor any other emotion that she felt; she was filled with the divine attribute of infinite indifference.

I am subjectively certain that some ancestor of mine with prognathous jaw, flat forehead and enormous thews, paddled over the sea that once filled these plains and roamed over the far-separated hill-tracks. I often saw him,—usually where the stark mountain range,—which in those old days was covered with verdure,—arises like a rampart from the northern limit of the plains. I have watched him crouching behind a rock with a sling in his hairy hand and a stone-axe slung to his girdle of twisted thongs,—his fierce eyes bent on a herd of Aurochs (or whatever the local contemporary equivalent of those beasts may have been) straying down to the entrance of a certain valley. There he had constructed, and skilfully concealed, a staked pit. The mountains at Agenhuis and the high kopjes at Gaams and Namies were then islands, and he used to paddle from one to the other in a canoe made of Aurochs' hide stretched over boughs. In the gorge that splits Agenhuis Mountain he waged mighty and victorious war with such dragons of the prime as attempted to lair therein,—for Agenhuis was one of his favourite sojourning places, and in the days when he flourished, dragons had not yet disappeared from earth.

In view of the undoubted scientific foundation upon which the germ-plasm theory rests, there is no limit to be set to atavistic memory. I am quite persuaded that this ancestor of mine actually existed; as a matter of fact I have over and over again seen him on the hunting trail, attending to the all-important business of filling his larder. I have watched him as he set forth in the early morning, empty and wrathful, and as he returned towards evening—still empty but laden with extraordinary spoil of antediluvian meat, and whooping an extempore triumphal chant.

He would fling the meat down at the mouth of his cave, and bellow for the attendance of his by-no-means gentle mate. She, with the fear of the stone-axe before her prehistoric eyes, would at once conceal the prehistoric baby in a corner, and with almost feverish energy busy herself with rudimentary cooking. A big fire would be already alight,—the embers containing stones in red-hot readiness for dropping into a pot-shaped depression in the cave's floor, half-full of water. Into this the meat and the stones would be flung together, but in the meantime a tit-bit had been lightly and hurriedly broiled, cleaned of ashes, and held out to the hunter on the end of a long stick, in a propitiatory way. After this had been snatched and swallowed to the accompaniment of savage growls, the cook seemed to be more at her ease. All this time the baby kept as still as a mouse. Prehistoric babies did not cry when papa was about, and hungry. In the exceptional cases where they did, it only happened once.

I trust my claim to such ancient lineage may not be put down to snobbery. One always suspects those who dwell unduly on the deeds of their ancestors. But my justification is this:—a germ charged with an epitome of that creature's stormy life has come down to me through the generations. It remained dormant until it met in my brain some solvent which disintegrated its shell and thus set the sleeper free. Garrulous after its long imprisonment the germ has told the story over and over again to all the grey molecules of my cortex. For some time most of these have known it off by heart.

Accordingly this ancestor—or perhaps for the sake of convenience I might term him my (many times removed) uncle—and I have been for some time shouting to each other across the ages, until we have attained to almost an intimacy. I have, in fact, by this means, acquired many prehistoric forms of thought. As may be imagined this has somewhat confused my ethical canons. Much of what I have learnt is difficult to translate into terms of modern speech.

I often long with all my soul to be prehistoric in certain matters, but the prim hand of convention—otherwise the unimaginative policeman—holds me back. However, some of my uncle's views are still more or less widely held. He was, for instance, what in modern speech would be called a strong Conservative; that is abundantly clear from many of his peculiarities. But in his day Imperialism had not yet been born; there was so far no urgent necessity to provide for the younger sons of the aristocracy. In fact there was still room in the world for everybody, and as cultivation had not yet been invented, there was no such thing as private ownership of land. Moreover, the pressure of over-population was never really felt until cannibalism went out of fashion, and that happened only quite recently.

My uncle was, of course, an aristocrat,—his three-fold patent of nobility being founded on his muscular strength, his skill in wielding weapons and his unique talent for concentrating all the faculties of his prehistoric mind on what I, his degenerate nephew, would call the main chance.

My aunt—there were several of them, of course, but you may take your choice, they were all of the same type—was an extremely practical woman. But she was not a Suffragette—or if she was she carefully concealed the circumstance. She was quite devoid of any kind of sentiment. In the matter of personal adornment, she affected the jewellery of the period; this consisted of the scalps and ears of my husband's deceased enemies—more or less dessicated—and the teeth of the same persons, bored through and strung on thin thongs. Her wardrobe was not extensive; in fact she never owned more than one garment at a time, and that she only used in cold weather. My uncle's hunting provided the material, so he had neither dressmakers' nor milliners' bills to meet.

My aunt was fiercely fond of her children so long as they depended upon her for food and protection. Afterwards she rather disliked them than otherwise. If one of them after reaching adolescence met her accidentally when she took her walks abroad, that one would utter a howl of dismay as loud as though he had met an angry odontosaurus, and flee, leaping from side to side to avoid the slung stones. For my aunt also carried a sling; she found it far more useful than a reticule.

How Nietsche would have delighted in this family; what a joy it would be to Mr Bernard Shaw. I can imagine my uncle dining with President Roosevelt,—but it would hardly have done to invite Booker Washington to meet him.

About two hours after midnight I coerced Andries into being merciful and calling a halt, for I felt that I must sleep or die. It was only when I had thrown myself prone on the sand and told Hendrick to picket the horses close by, that Andries relented. There was really no object in pushing on at such rapid rate; by making an early start we could easily reach Gamoep shortly after noon on the morrow.

Both Danster and Piet Noona reported the presence of springbuck in this vicinity. Mrs Esterhuizen would be disappointed and contemptuous if we returned without meat other than the half-dried oryx-flesh. When, I again asked myself, would repentance for the crimes I committed in slaying those beautiful desert creatures become final and practical, instead of intermittent? Saint Augustine once put up a prayer for the grace of continence, but added a rider to the effect that he did not desire it to be granted immediately. This somewhat suggested my state of mind. But I meant some day to lay down my rifle finally—perhaps after a particularly good bag or an unusually skilful shot. Afterwards I should never kill another animal—unless in self-defence or because I badly lacked meat. However, in the meantime, like Saint Augustine, I knew I should continue certain practices which my conscience reprehended. The hunter's instinct is the one most deeply rooted in the mind of man; it is among those tendencies which persist after the conditions which called them forth have disappeared—even from memory. It is the true basis of that original sin over which the theologians fumble, for in the absence of other available game men hunt each other.

But I had, incontinently, to sleep. And hey—for a gallop over the plains in the morning.

Chapter Seven.

The Springbuck Drive—The Bushman Caves—Return to Gamoep.

Morning,—and the cool west wind, laden with refreshment, hastened over the desert's rim to where I lay, still on the border-land of sleep. The sweeping garments of the air-spirit were fragrant with the ichor of the sea on whose breast it had slept. Its sandals whispered through the swaying tussocks, its tresses trailed over the bending plumes of the "toa" shocks. It gently tried to draw me back to the mistress I loved and longed for, but was deserting because she would have slain me had I lingered at her unpitying feet.

At sunrise I gazed around for one ecstatic moment and again sank to sleep—to a zone too deep for dreams to haunt. The long trampings of the previous two nights had made further slumber an almost absolute necessity. Andries might go hang; I would not move.

The grateful aroma of coffee wakened me. I decided to breakfast in bed; that is without emerging from my kaross. Andries determined to go on with the wagon. Hendrick and the horses were to remain with me; also Piet Noona's nephew who would, later, trot on and overtake the wagon with my kaross and pannikin. After another hour's sleep the sun became insupportable, for the wind had somewhat died down, so I ordered my faithful Hun to saddle up. He had already located a herd of springbuck. It had been settled that we were to try and drive these near enough to the track to afford Andries some shooting. No one but Hendrick had seen the game; he said they were too far off—away, ahead,—on the left-hand side of the track,—for us to see. Andries was to lie in ambush at a certain knoll, while the wagon went on to Kanxas,—there to be outspanned.

Hendrick's powers of vision were phenomenal; when objects at a distance were in question, no one dreamt of disputing his verdict. His eyes were equal, if not superior to the best prismatic binoculars ever turned out by Dollond or Zeiss, and Nature had apparently corrected them for chromatic and all other aberrations.

The western hills could now be distinctly seen; we might even recognise the contours of the ridge beyond the northern end of which Gamoep lay. Soon we should pass from the kingdom of ancient silence to where the squalid tents of nomadic men were temporarily pitched,—to where the fat-tailed sheep crowded, with anxious eyes, around the creaking derrick and the scanty trough. But to us, intruders as we were, the desert had still to pay tribute.

We started, Hendrick and I, riding quietly forth on a course a little to the east of south, for we had a wide détour to make. I knew the vicinity well; it was, literally speaking, a part of the desert, but I found it hard to acknowledge it as such, for the reason that the western hills were in sight. These seemed to link us with the conventional world.

We passed over a tract studded with small, dense patches of low scrub; it looked like a miniature archipelago in the boundless ocean of "toa." Here brown "duiker" antelopes were numerous. So far as I knew this was the only part of Bushmanland where such were to be found. As we rode on the little creatures sprang out, right and left, from the patches of cover and bounded gracefully away.

Far to the south-west the herd of springbuck was now clearly visible. Most of them were quietly grazing in the mild sunshine. Now and then a few detached themselves from the main body and, one behind the other, bounded away for a few hundred yards on a course curved like the blade of a scimitar—"pronking" with the sheer joy of unspoilt life. After such an excursion they would rejoin the others and go on feeding. And I had come to... But if I had let Jekyll climb to my crupper Andries would have got no shooting. The herd was a small one; it did not number more than about six hundred. It was curious that these bucks had not joined in the general migration eastward towards where the lightning had flashed its message of rain a few nights previously.

The springbucks had not seen us as yet, for we were still about two miles distant from them. The eyes of these animals seem to be specialised to a definite range as the ear is tuned to a certain gamut of sound. I will endeavour to explain what is meant by this. They do not seem to notice anything at a greater distance than about fifteen hundred yards. Conversely, should you be lying in ambush and the bucks come to within fifty yards of you, they would evince far less alarm if you shewed yourself than on seeing you at a distance of from two to three hundred yards.

This can easily be accounted for. The springbuck has always spent its life in an environment of menace, but as conditions change the nature of the menace changes with them. Formerly the danger-zone for these creatures was that from which the lion, the leopard or the wild dog could spring; it was only surprise at close quarters that the springbuck had to guard against. Given a few seconds' notice of the approach of an enemy, this creature's unsurpassed fleetness enabled it to laugh at danger. This laughter is still expressed in the manner in which a small herd of springbuck will circle round and round a pursuing dog that is not especially swift—as porpoises sometimes circle around a moving ship.

We know from accounts left by the very old hunters that in early days, when the killing range of a bullet was little more than a hundred yards, springbuck would graze with apparent unconcern until approached to within about that distance. But with the disappearance of the larger carnivora before firearms, and the increase in the range of the rifle, a wider danger-zone has been created, while the danger of an enemy at close quarters has practically disappeared. The width of the danger-zone has gone on increasing with the longer range of the rifle.

Wild animals are quick to learn and to unlearn—which is not quite the same as to forget. Thus the springbuck has ceased to dread the springing enemy, the creature of teeth and claws that used to lie in ambush; in fact he never contemplates the contingency of any enemy at close quarters, and on the rare occasions when he meets one, the experience appears to fill him with surprise rather than alarm.

The distance between us and the herd had decreased to a little over two thousand yards, so I detached Hendrick and instructed him to alter his course to the left and endeavour to edge round the still unsuspecting animals. The object was to stampede the herd so that it would pass me on my right and head towards where Andries lay in ambush. Bucephalus and Hendrick loomed immense and black against the background of yellow shocks, but they were apparently unobserved by the game, for the latter still grazed and "pronked" about as though they had the whole desert to themselves,—as though no entangling web were being drawn about them.

Hendrick had reached the limit of his arc; then the springbuck marked him and evidently realised that there was danger. Apprehension touched them; a quiver ran through the herd; they lifted their heads and gazed; they moved to and fro. So far it was not fear that they felt; for they knew their own fleetness and had trust in it. Then, suddenly, terror seemed to strike them like a blast, for as dead leaves are caught by a wind-eddy and whirled in a spiral, these imponderable-seeming, ethereal desert creatures swerved over an area resembling in form the sweep of a fan, and then streamed forth like a handful of white rose-petals before a gale.

Why is it, I wonder, that during the forenoon springbuck in the desert appear to be white? For this is literally the case; these animals seemed to be as white as snow, as imponderable as thistledown. The fawn-tint of their necks and flanks, the broad, brown patches on their sides, the black, lyre-formed horns,—all were drowned in the milky foam of the dorsal manes. These were expanded laterally to their fullest extent; each long silvery hair stood erect and quivering.

The creatures' heads were depressed almost to the level of their feet. With backs deeply arched they bounded over the face of the desert like so many alabaster discs—mingling, separating and re-combining in a tracery of flying arabesques. They had adopted the attitude and movement usual to their kind in moments of sudden terror or delight. Surely their flight was the highest

41

expression of grace revealed by animated nature in motion. It was a soundless melody; a symphony for the eye.

The torrent was streaming to my right, straight for Andries. Hendrick thundered behind,—a black Centaur-monstrosity. How terrible he must have appeared to the fugitives. I wished Hendrick then would trend to *his* right, for if the springbuck had swerved towards Kanxas and caught sight of the wagon, they would have doubled on their tracks and made for the depths of the desert. My object was to hold them on the course they were following for as long as possible. Ha! they must have sighted the wagon, for they wheeled to their right and attempted to escape past me, about three thousand yards on my side of where Andries lay waiting for his shot. The terror of death was upon them; their manes were down—hidden in the constricted dorsal tract. The eye could hardly follow the movement of their limbs; distance died beneath the lightning of their feet.

The reins fell upon my horse's neck, I pressed my spurless heels to his sides; he knew what was required of him. We dashed forward to cut the herd off. While we had to cover a thousand yards the springbuck had to cover nearly two—yet it was clear that they must win the race. When the springbuck runs his best the speed he attains is almost incredible. There remained but one thing to be done.

After having altered my course so as to reach some slightly higher ground, I rolled from the saddle on to the soft sand and began firing—not at the bucks, but so that my bullets would strike some twenty or thirty yards in front of the leaders of the herd. Bullet after bullet scarred the ground, sending up spouts of red sand—now here, now there. The herd faltered in bewilderment, whirled round in a half-circle to the left, and headed straight for the ambush.

A distant shot—another; several in rapid succession. It was the rifle of Andries speaking. It was Man taking toll of Nature, imposing his age-long tribute of blood and pain. It was Death eliminating Beauty become obsolete. It was like Autumn shedding the petals of a flower that had lived its allotted day.

The hunted creatures, in their dismay, completed the circle of frantic effort; they sped back to the spot where they had been disturbed. They passed it; they grew smaller and smaller until they melted into the infinite mystery of the desert.

Three bucks had fallen to Andries' rifle. I dismounted, and we piled the carcases on Prince's patient back. Bucephalus, as usual, grew frantic on being brought within smelling-distance of the slain game. Then we strolled to where the wagon was waiting for us, at a spot some three miles away, close to the head of the Kanxas Gorge. There we dined sumptuously on roasted springbuck liver,—one of the best of desert delicacies.

Once more I explored the gorge—that deserted city which once teemed with human life. It was narrow, it was neither long nor deep; a mere scar it was on the desert's flank. The greatest depth was not more than fifty feet; it was possibly a mile long and the width varied. The sides contained caves, on the walls of which could still be seen traces of fires lit long, long ago. And there, thickly traced on the ledges was the mysterious, black-pigmented script—the groups of short, diagonal lines crossing each other at various angles. What did they indicate; was nothing to be read from them even by those who deciphered the graven edict, five-and-twenty centuries old, of Mesha the Sheepmaster?

Why was it that one did not find at Kanxas pictures of the eland, the oryx and the rhinoceros; why were there no perspectiveless battle-pieces depicting the successful defence of some cave-stronghold, with the baffled invaders being hurled down precipices? Such pictures are found distributed over vast areas of South Eastern Africa; it seemed remarkable that none exist, so far as I am aware, in Bushmanland.

Perhaps the plants from which the necessary pigments had to be extracted do not grow on that side of South Africa. But, deep in the Orange River gorge is a continuous strip of rich and varied woodland, in which most of the South African forest flora is represented. Moreover, on the islands which gem the river's course near its mouth are to be found myriads of eastern plants, the progeny of seeds carried down by the annual flood from far-off Basutoland and its environs,—and it is precisely in that vicinity that Bushman paintings are most plentiful. The thing remains a puzzle.

And the strange, highly-evolved dramatic art of that vanished race,—a drama in which human beings took the parts of animals,—how often had it not found expression there in days of bygone plenty; days when the baskets of dried-locust cakes crowded every ledge and the children went pot-bellied and sleek.

There was the stage; there the auditorium; yonder the ledge along which, no doubt, the actors made their exits and their entrances. Was the audience a critical one; did it generously applaud a nervous new actor of evident talent; did it hurl stones, at one who bungled his part or tried to make up in pretentiousness what he lacked in ability? Did the author of a successful play advance to the proscenium and enjoy the tribute of plaudits paid to a successful playwright?

I fancy there must have been a chorus; possibly a semi-chorus as well. Thespis and Aeschylus probably adopted those obvious aids to rudimentary drama from the shepherd,—who is first-cousin to the savage. And the more one sees of various savages, belong they to Bushmanland or to the Bowery, the more astonishing is the kinship revealed between them. I could find no box-office— no gallery from which the gods could have jibed. The auditorium must have been all pit.

And what dramas of real life must have been enacted in that rocky valley; what rudimentary idylls had not the moon looked upon as her slanting beams searched slowly down among the rocks on summer nights. There men and women loved; there jealousy, cruel as the grave, had brooded. There vengeance had stalked abroad and taken toll for Fate. Finally, from there—after an age-long struggle—Death had evicted Life. It was, after all, only appropriate that the Kanxas fountain should have ceased to flow.

How often had not some old lion—some gaunt, lonely brute with blunted teeth and claws worn to the quick, crouched among those rocks, bent on spoil of the cave-men? During how many nights of livid fear must not the horrible purring

43

of the man-eater, as he quested up the gorge, have sunk to the deadlier horror of silence. For then every member of the little community would have known that the prowler had at length selected a dwelling from which presently to drag a shrieking victim.

And later, the arch-enemy, the more cruel spoiler, man. Man—the spoiler to-day,—to-morrow the spoiled. The European revenged the Bushman on the Hottentot; who would revenge the Hottentot on the European? "For that which hath been is, and that which will be hath been, and there is no new thing." The thought made "a goblin of the sun." "O stars that sway our fate; O orbs that should be very wise, for you have circled the heavens and regarded the earth from the most ancient days,—you who, impassively, have seen an endless succession of civilisations arise, decline and die,—when, and at whose hand, will our nemesis come?"

A spirit of laziness had overcome us all. Andries lay fast asleep under the wagon; his large frame was loosened, his placid, handsome, weather-beaten face relaxed. He would have looked just as he did then, had he been dead, for his days had been days of quietness and all his pathways peaceful. Yet in that man's deliberate arteries flowed the blood of those who withstood Alva in the Netherlands, and of others who abandoned France, with all that seemed to make life worth the living, rather than bend the knee at the shrine of a false god. I wondered whether that large-boned, contented, easy-going farmer were capable of standing on the ramparts of another Leyden and, from hunger-bitten, indomitable lips roaring heroic and vitriolic defiance at a seemingly-unconquerable foe. Would he have abandoned honour, riches, comfort, roof-tree and friends for the sake of conscience,—that discipliner whose whip-lash does not, unfortunately, bite as severely as it once was wont to do? I wondered, and in wondering breathed one of those wishes which are the essence of prayer, that he might never be put to the test.

The afternoon was young. I decided to stroll on, ahead. I found Danster and Piet Noona's nephew just above the krantz—preventing, with some difficulty, the oxen from stampeding to Gamoep, which was now only about ten miles distant. I sent them back to the wagon with instructions to do the thing my heart had failed of,—to waken a human being from that highest condition of well-being—perfect sleep. But it was now time to inspan; for the first time since they had last drunk the oxen were really suffering from thirst. They, too, had their rights. Andries, moreover, was one of those fortunate beings who could slumber at will.

So I again strolled on. I left the track and climbed to the top of the Koeberg, the hill from which the big beacon—that farthest outpost of the trigonometrical survey on this side—springs like a startled finger. This was one of the actual portals of the desert. I was now, alas! once more within sight of the dwellings of men. Several tents had been pitched, and quite a number of mat-houses set up at Gamoep since we had left it, a little more than a week previously.

I turned eastward and cast mournful eyes back over the sun-bathed immensity from which I had emerged, and from the deepest depths of which sounded a call

44

that I knew would for ever echo in my soul. What a strange regret it was that tugged at my aching heartstrings...

The wind had here died down. The morrow would be torrid,—perhaps with a tornado from the north. As the last skirts of the sea-cooled breeze trailed away into the infinite east, their track was marked by a line of towering sand-spouts. So gently did these move across the plains that it seemed as though they stood like a row of lofty columns sustaining the temple-dome of the sky. Yet a careful eye might detect their rhythmic and concerted movement. What was the stately measure they were treading,—to what sphere-music did their gliding feet keep time?

And then, O desert—O steadfast face that I loved—I had to bid you farewell. These eyes would gaze upon you again, but the day was swiftly coming when I should have to take leave of you for ever. But if when the body dies the spirit still lives, this soul which was nourished by your hand until it grew to a stature sufficient to enable it to realise its own littleness, will return and merge itself in your immensity.

Chapter Eight.

The Summer Clouds—News of Rain—Start for Pella—The Vedic Hymns—Digging for Water—Arrival at Pella—Terrible Heat—The Tribe—Aquinas in the Wilderness—The Mission—The River Gorge—The Tarantula Invasion.

That mountain tract stretching like a back-bone through Namaqualand, parallel with the coast upon which the Atlantic ceaselessly thunders, is the region which catches the sparse, south-western winter rains,—but which in summer is the abode of drought. On the in-lying Bushmanland plains the winters are quite arid; it is only in summer, when occasional thunderstorms stray down from the north-east, that the level desert gets rain.

In a season when the Storm Gods go forth mightily to war on the aether seas, and the capricious heavens are bountiful, it is a striking experience to climb, on a torrid afternoon, some peak jutting from the eastern margin of the mountain tract, and from there to watch the ordered procession of the thunder-ships as they sweep down from their far-off port of assembly. Like great battle-craft, black beneath and equipped with dreadful artillery,—their dazzling decks heaped and laden with ocean-gleaned merchandise of crudded white,—they charge menacingly across the illimitable plains as though to overwhelm the granite ranges. But each stately vessel barely touches some outlying buttress; then the aery hull swerves and changes its course due south, bearing its most precious freight to more fortunate regions. It is as though some immense, invisible fender were being lowered from the sky to guard the range from the shock of impact.

There came good news from Bushmanland; thunderstorm after thunder-storm had trailed over the plains, each marking its path with verdure and filling every rock-depression with water. The drought had broken, so my long-postponed trip to Pella, that remote outpost of French-Roman Catholicism, could be undertaken. Pella lies where the iron mountains, like a leash of black panthers, spring from the northern margin of the plains,—and then sink to their lair in that great gorge through whose depths the Orange River swirls and eddies with its drainage of a million hills.

We were to travel with horses along a route I had special reasons for wishing to take, but which, had the drought still prevailed, we would not have dared to traverse. But under the existing circumstances it would never be necessary to travel more than twenty miles without finding a spot where a water-pit might be dug.

So Andries brought his spring-wagon in to the Copper Mines and we made busy preparations for a start. Our wagon-team numbered eight, four belonging to Andries and four to me. Old Prince pulled as a wheeler; my two young chestnuts as leaders. Besides the wagon we had another vehicle,—a strange, springless, nondescript contraption knocked together by Andries out of the remains of an old horse-wagon which he had broken up. It had low, strong wheels set very wide apart, with a rough framework of yellow-wood boards superimposed. There was no seat, but a box-like rim of woodwork edged the frame. To this vehicle four half-trained horses were yoked. It was intended to be used in pursuing springbuck over the plains. Hendrick was to be the driver; his task would not be an easy one. Andries owned a mob of over sixty horses, the greater number of which had been taught but the merest rudiments of service.

We reached the outer periphery of the hills late in the afternoon, and camped on the margin of the pale-green ocean of feathery "toa." Far-off, to eastward, we marked the rose-litten turrets of a thunder-cloud. When the sun went down these were illuminated by incessant lightnings, symbols of destruction heralding the advent of the only giver of life-rain.

I had formerly been accustomed to bring books to Bushmanland, but, with one exception, I did so no longer. The exception was Ludwig's translation of the Vedic Hymns. The open Volume of the desert, so insistent to be read, was sufficient; nevertheless those large, primordial utterances of the Vedas seemed appropriate whenever one was brought into contact with unspoilt Nature in her vaster aspects. Although they originated under conditions very dissimilar to the local ones, the Vedic Hymns are tuned to the desert's pitch. In India, as in Bushmanland, rain is the paramount necessity. When the rain-gods forget Bushmanland a few thousand fat-tailed sheep may perish; a hundred families may have to retire from its margins and live for a season by digging wild tubers among the granite hills, or by robbing the ants of their underground store of "toa" seed. But if a similar thing happen in India, perhaps ten millions of human beings die a horrible death.

In the desert,—away from man and everything that suggested him, the Hebrew Scriptures seemed to be too overloaded with ethics, too exigent towards enlisting the services of the deity on the side of tribe against tribe. But the Vedic Hymnist was a worshipper who imposed no conditions upon his gods. He had passionately realised the fundamental fact that his own continued existence, as well as that of all organic life, depended upon the beneficent fury of the sky, so he offered awed and unconditioned adoration to Indra, Agni and the "golden-breasted" Storm Gods through a symbolism of sincere and homely dignity. Submissive, he accepted death or life, the thunder-bolt or the Soma-flower,—the drought that slew its millions or the rain that brought a bounteous harvest.

We started at break of day. Although rain had fallen, we felt it necessary to plan our course carefully, for water was only to be found in the sand-covered rock-depressions—and these, albeit more than ordinarily frequent in that section of the desert over which our route lay, were nevertheless few and far between. The weather was hot; therefore the horses, unlike oxen, had to drink at least once a day. Even where it existed, water could only be obtained by digging to a depth of from five to eight feet; then it had to be scooped up in pannikins after having trickled in from the sides and collected at the bottom of the pit. Thus, even under favourable conditions, it took about two hours' hard work to provide sufficient water to quench the thirst of twelve animals.

With cocked ears and anxious looks the horses would crowd to where the smell of wet sand told them that relief was near; it became necessary to keep them off with a whip. Once I narrowly escaped being badly hurt owing to a mule flinging itself into a pit in which I was digging for water.

We decided not to delay on our forward journey; therefore the various herds of game seen in the distance were not interfered with. We intended, after finishing our business at Pella, to seek out some temporary oasis favourably situated, pitch our camp there and spend a few days shooting in the vicinity.

On the forenoon of the fourth day,—a day of terrible heat, we sighted the mission buildings of Pella in the far distance. These stood on a limestone ridge in a crescent-shaped bend of that stark range of mountains on the northern side of which the Orange River has carved its tremendous earth-scar. Here the colour of the mountains changed; they were no longer jet-black as I had found those a hundred miles to westward, but a deep chocolate brown. From Pella ran a steep ravine which cleft the range almost to its base. Down this a crooked track led to the river, which was said to be about nine miles away.

It seemed as though we should never reach the mission; the trek over red-hot sand through which angular chunks of limestone were thickly distributed, seemed interminable in the fierce heat. But at length the journey ended, and the panting horses were released for their sand-bath, preliminary to a much-needed drink. The half-dozen low houses of the mission, built of unburnt brick and livid-grey in colour, lay huddled around the unfinished walls of what was intended to eventually be a church. That bare, sun-scourged, glaring ridge which had been selected as the site for the institution lacked every attribute tempting to man—save one: and that the all-essential,—water. For thither, to the midst of a howling desolation, Nature, in one of her moods of whimsical paradox, had enticed from the depths a spring of living crystal. Through torrid day and frosty night,—through short, adventitious rainy season and long, inevitable period of aridity which filled man and brute with dismay,—"ohne hast, ohne rast" the gentle fountain welled out, cold and clear. It seemed as though some spirit whose dwelling was deep in a zone untroubled by the moods of the changeful sky stretched forth a pitiful hand to touch the scarred forehead of the waste with comfort and with healing.

47

The heat in the wagon had been a burthen and almost a misery, yet I was able to sustain it while we were in motion. But the stillness of the atmosphere and the glare from the limestone surrounding the mission, made one desperate. Shade—coolness—where were they to be found? Even mere darkness would have been a relief. I sought refuge under a verandah, but got no assuagement. I longed for some corner into which to creep—for somewhere to hide, if only from the blistering light. Father Simon, the Director of the Mission, kindly vacated his house and placed it at my disposal. The building contained but one room.

I entered and closed the door. For a few seconds the darkness brought a sense of easement, but the closeness, the thick stagnation of the air, made me gasp. And the heat was nearly as bad as it was outside. How was that? I put my hand to one of the clod-like bricks of which the walls were built. It was quite uncomfortably hot to the touch; the force of the sun had penetrated it.

Something approaching despair seized me; it was then nearly noon—could I live through another six hours of such torture? I began to speculate as to what were the initial symptoms of heat-apoplexy. The labouring blood thundered in my ears; I felt perilously near delirium. It was as though one were being suffocated in the cellar of a burning house. I stripped off my clothes and grovelled naked on the clay floor, seeking relief in cobwebby corners. In the gloom I caught sight of a bucket of water. I tore a sheet from the bed, soaked it and wrapped it around me. In all my life I had never felt in such physical extremity. However, lying on the ground wrapped in the wet sheet brought a measure of relief. But the miseries of that day will never be forgotten.

At length the sun went down—sank in golden ruin among the fang-like peaks of the umber-tinted western mountains. Soon the quivering earth flung off its Nessus-garment and a delicious interval followed. But shortly after nightfall the chilliness of the air became so uncomfortable that I overhauled my belongings in the wagon, seeking a warmer coat. Father Simon, with a smile, produced his thermometer; the mercury stood at 86 Fahrenheit. I learned that five hours previously it had reached 119 in the shade.

Next day brought practically no diminution of temperature; but somehow I seemed to have acquired resisting power. The fear of possible collapse, even of death, which came upon me the previous day, had gone. Perhaps the fatigues of the long journey—more especially the heavy digging in the water-pits—may have lowered my vitality. Presently we had another severe ordeal to undergo, for we decided to make our way down the gorge and spend a night on the bank of the river. It seemed as though it would be like descending to the Gehenna-pit.

But first to bend an examining eye upon that strange community of men and women,—those adventurers from the Old World to a world immeasurably older and less changeful. So far as I could gather, the personnel consisted of three priests, four lay-brothers and five nuns. It was to those women that my pity went out; they were so pallid, so debilitated,—so incongruous with their surroundings. As they flitted silently about, busied with hospitable service towards the guests, their hands looked like faded leaves. How the conventual habit, albeit the material had been lightened to accord with local conditions, must have weighed them down. The low-roofed, livid-grey brick building in

48

which they lived must have got heated through and through as Father Simon's dwelling did. One of those nuns had, so I was told, lost her reason and was shortly to be removed. Their lot must have been one of continuous martyrdom.

Father Simon was suave in manner; I could judge him to be shrewd and clear-headed; evidently he was a man of affairs. His pallor was apparently congenital; it by no means suggested physical weakness. Salamander-like, he had habituated himself to the torrid climate. Like an Arab chief he ruled his clan of about two hundred subjects. This was as mixed a lot of human beings as one would find anywhere—even in South Africa, that land of varied human blends. Among them were pure-bred Europeans,—some bearing names held in honour from Cape Town to Pretoria. Others were frankly black,—and there were all intermediate shades.

Just then the mat-houses of the tribe were pitched at one of the outlying water-places; I did not learn how far off, for distance is an unimportant detail in the desert. But it was some place where a thunderstorm had recently burst and, therefore, where pasturage existed. The wealth of the community consisted of fat-tailed sheep, horses, goats and a few cattle. The Pella lands were held by the Mission on ownership tenure; consequently the Superintendent was an autocrat. A community of that kind was as little fitted to govern itself as a reformatory would have been. The territory over which Father Simon held sway contained all the water-places which were to be found in that corner of the desert. The water in some of these was permanent, the severest drought occasioning no diminution in its flow. It was this circumstance, more than anything else, which rendered the autocracy effective.

Acceptance of the forms of the Roman Catholic ritual was the only condition of membership; faith appeared to be taken on trust. It was told me that when Bushmanland happened to be blest with a few consecutive good seasons, scruples on points of dogma became prevalent and the tribe thinned out. But when the inevitable drought recurred, the doubters repented, returned to the forgiving bosom of Mother Church and recommenced, with more or less fervour, the practice of their religious duties. I was shewn one patriarch who, with his numerous family, had three times fallen from grace and had as often been received back as an erring but repentant sheep.

Besides Father Simon and the nuns I met only two members of the community who interested me. One was an elderly, thickset priest with a dense, brown beard. I found him sitting, in a dingy hut, at a packing-case table. He was smoking an extremely black pipe and reading at an early 17th Century folio of Thomas Aquinas. His person was generally unclean; his coarse, stumpy hands were sickening to look upon.

The reading was clearly a pretence; from the appearance of the volume I should say it had not been previously opened for a very long time. I felt instinctively that Father Simon, too, knew this, for he addressed a few sentences in French to the reader,—speaking in a low, even, firm voice. At once the folio was closed and put back on a cobwebby shelf.

WHERE THE IRON MOUNTAINS LIKE A LEASH OF BLACK PANTHERS SPRING FROM THE DESERT'S NORTHERN MARGE

The episode interested me; I sympathised with that priest. In spite of his unsavoury physical condition my heart went out to him. His life must have been appallingly empty, for he had not, like Father Simon, the saving grace of responsibility and the opportunity of expressing his individuality in administrative work. He was nothing but a more or less superfluous cog in the wheel of a cranky machine driven by a despotic hand. The Adam within him cried out for an opportunity of attracting the attention of the only visitor from the outside world he was likely to see for the next six months. I found that little trifle of deception very human—very pitiful. I wonder did he, after all, read his Aquinas at times; perhaps he did. But I fear his development would rather have been in the direction of the "dumb ox" than towards the angels. Poor, lonely, unwashed human creature.

The only way to save one's soul alive in the desert is to wrestle with and overcome difficulties—as Jacob wrestled with the angel, and all the cobwebs ever spun by all the Schoolmen would not give so much strength to the human spirit as a gallop of ten miles over the plains, among the whispering shocks of the "toa." That this was the case was evinced by a young lay-brother with whom I was able to converse in Dutch. He, of peasant origin and with quite a lot of fire glowing through his clay, found scope for his abounding energies in looking after the stock belonging to the Mission and generally carrying on the outside administrative work. It was he who shepherded the tribe from one water-place to another; it was he who took venturesome journeys across wide stretches of desert for the purpose of reporting as to the condition of the pasturage surrounding the far-outlying oases.

This man was brown and muscular; his eye was steady and masterful— because his life was spent in action, not in futile dreaming. If he should have looked upon one of the daughters of the desert and found her fair, I would not have given much for his vocation. I sincerely hoped he might do so. The daughters of the desert are not, as a rule, comely—but, after all, beauty is relative. I imply nothing discreditable; this man had taken no irrevocable vow of celibacy.

The Pella Mission was engaged in the hopeless task of endeavouring to make oil and water mix—or rather, to change the metaphor—to graft an archaic but vigorous and highly-specialised organism upon a rudimentary one of thin blood and low vitality. A creed rooted in and nourished by the most ancient human traditions could not possibly develop among people who possessed no traditions and had not enough positive original sin in them to make their asthenic souls worth the saving.

On this desert tract where men are blown to and fro by the fiery breath of recurrent drought, they should be left to sink in the sand or swim in the aether,—to develop body and soul of a tenacious fibre, or else to be eliminated by the adverse conditions under which they exist. Subject to tuition, kept erect by outside support, they must presently stagnate and ultimately perish. From my point of view their preservation was not nearly so important as that of the herd of oryx I was endeavouring to protect from its legioned enemies in central Bushmanland.

But the case of the Pella tribe was hopeless. Could these people have gone to war, had the desert they inhabited been ten times as wide and had its bounds contained tribes that raided one another, and thus made valour-cum-skill-in-arms the alternative to extinction, they might have developed positive virtues and vices. They might even have lifted their eyes to the stars and uttered songs of love and death.

The blistering sun of noon was almost over our heads when we started on our pilgrimage to the river. A crooked pathway choked with sand, into which one's feet sank deep at every step, led down the wedge-formed cleft between the towering mountains. We found the course fatiguing in the descent; what would it be when we came to retrace our steps? As we proceeded the gorge bent to the right and the glowing cliffs closed in.

At length the stupendous mountain range on the other side of the river again sprang into view. Soon we caught a glimpse of the rich-green forest strip which fringed, on either side, the wide course of the stream. There at least we would find shade. The heat had become frightful; it was as though one breathed flame.

We reached the river bank. The great torrent of a few weeks back had shrunk to a network of rivulets which swirled and eddied among the rocks and islanded sand-banks with a soothing murmur. The trees just there had been much thinned out; in places the undergrowth had completely disappeared,—eaten away by the stock which was sent thither in seasons of exceptional drought. A recent freshet had carpeted the shaded ground with soft, white sand. A dip in the tepid water refreshed one; the gentle, lapping wavelets whispered of coolness to come. But the river, so gentle that day, could at times arise like a wrathful Titan. In a high cliff-crevice hung a large tree-trunk flung up and wedged there during some recent flood.

Who could paint the terrific desolation of that home of chaos,—the towering peaks, the jutting ledges, the Cyclopean, bulging protuberances? That

51

amphitheatre was surely the haunt of some ferocious, inimical Nature-spirit—brother to Death and a hater of Life. Yet life flourished even here, for the river, like a mother holding her children with tender clasp, led westward her progeny of trees over strait and perilous pathways. But the feet of the brood dared not stray from the hem of her garment.

The sun sank; as the glare was withdrawn each salient detail of the Titanic arena grew clearer and more definite against the background of darkening blue. Then shadow gathered all into her fold, and it was upon a pit whose black sides threatened to fall in and crush us, that the stars of the zenith looked down.

It was deep in the night, but the heat still raged, for the sides of the glowing rock-pit in which we lay continued to radiate what energy they had absorbed while the sun still smote on them. We had emerged from among the trees and built a large fire of drift-wood on a sandbank,—our object being to obtain illumination. It was quite necessary to have a bright light; from many of the logs poisonous centipedes, and an occasional scorpion, were emerging. But even comparatively close to the fire we could feel no increase of heat. My gun stood against a stone some distance away. I picked the weapon up, but involuntarily dropped it, for the barrel almost scorched my hand. And this at nearly midnight!

But what were those creatures darting here and there; anon rushing towards us over the livid surface of the sand? Horror. They were tarantulas,—red, hairy creatures, larger than mice. Within a few seconds there were hundreds of them circling around the fire with almost incredible swiftness. The firelight had attracted them from the cliff-chasms which yawned around us.

This was too much for flesh and blood to endure, so I beat a retreat to the river and waded out until I reached a flat rock. This proved to be uncomfortably hot, but the soles of my boots were thick, and I could every now and then cool them in the water. However, a few yards away lay a small island of sand, and on this I took refuge. From my retreat I could see the fire and its environs. I did not think Africa contained so many tarantulas as were then visible. They had the fire to themselves, for every member of the party had fled.

The air still felt as though one were in a closed room. But the murmur of the river became audible to an increasing degree on the western side, and soon a hot breath of air struck us. After a fitful succession of puffs a continuous wind set in,—a steady current, momentarily growing cooler. This was the sea-breeze stealing up the river gorge from the far-off Atlantic, rolling the mass of heated air before it and cooling the piled rocks,—helping them to fling off the yoke of torment put upon them by the cruel, arrogant sun. Soon the temperature began to fall rapidly, so I waded back, made a wide détour so as to avoid the tarantula-infested area, and fetched my kaross from where it lay among the trees. I then returned to my sand-islet and there sank into blessed sleep with the tepid water murmuring within a few feet of my weary head.

I awoke soon after 3 a.m. The wind had turned perishingly cold,—so cold that I decided to retire from my exposed situation and seek for some spot more or less sheltered from the streaming air-current. So I once more waded back through the tepid water and sought a refuge among the trees. The fire was still alight; I had to pass it. Not a single tarantula was visible; no doubt they had retired to their lairs among the rocks on account of the fall in the temperature. Yet I do not suppose the latter was below 80 Fahrenheit; the susceptibility of one's skin is relative; my discomfort was due to the sudden change. I wished I had not left my thermometer at the wagon; it would have been interesting to take a reading at midnight.

Once more I fell asleep, with the tree-trunks groaning around me, as the boughs swayed in the ever-freshening gale.

Chapter Nine.

Morning in the Gorge—Departure from Pella—Journey to Brabies—Protection of the Oryx—Its Peculiarities—Antelopes of the Desert and the Forest—Camping at Brabies.

Daybreak,—and the chill sea-wind was still surging up the gorge. It was delightful; nevertheless, even among the sheltering trees, a fire was very comforting. The pageant of growing day was a wonder and a delight. The upper tiers of that titanic rock-city became glorious "under the opening eyelids of the morn." They were refulgent with hitherto unsuspected beauty. Those acre-large splashes of vermilion, blue and amber-brown must have been due to lichen. It was strange that on the previous evening we had not noticed these. Perhaps they paled under the flames of day and only revived when the cool, moist sea-wind bathed them.

After a hurried dip in the still-tepid water, followed by breakfast, we started on our journey back to Pella. The wind sank momentarily, but the air was still deliciously cool, for the bow of the sun-archer could not yet be depressed enough to send its searching arrows into the depths of the cleft through which our course lay. Soon the sea-wind folded its wings; not a breath stirred. From their eyries in the towering rock bastions the brown eagles swooped down as though to rend us, uttering wild and menacing cries.

The relentless sunbeams searched ever lower upon the western face of the chasm. From the crannies gorgeous-hued lizards crept forth to bask. Their lovely colours—vivid crimson or deep, gentian blue seemed incongruous with their ungainly form and ferocious expression. Here and there rock-rabbits darted from ledge to ledge. Crossing our sandy pathway we occasionally noticed the spoor of a leopard, a badger or a snake. For such creatures night is the season of activity; by day they could choose the climate best suited to them,—among the deep, dark cavern-clefts with which this tumbled chaos is honeycombed.

We were now beyond the area of shade; no longer did the cliff protect us. For an hour we laboured up the widening gorge, over the yielding sand,—in the glaring, unmitigated sunshine. It was with a grateful sense of relief that we reached Pella, somewhat breathless, but none the worse for our adventure.

The teams were soon inspanned, so after thanking Father Simon and the nuns for their kind entertainment, and paying a farewell visit to the student of Aquinas in his dingy hut, we made a start for Brabies,—"the place of the withered flower," as the Bushmen named it. At Brabies it was that we had decided to pitch our hunting camp, for we heard good reports as to the water in the vley there. No one, so far as we knew, had been there lately, but a heavy thunderstorm had been observed to pass over the vicinity of Brabies about a week previously. Our objective was about thirty miles away. There was a slight improvement in the weather. The cool spell of the distant sea, owing to last night's wind, still lay upon the grateful desert.

We pushed on steadily but could not travel fast, for the sand was heavy and the angular limestone fragments lay thick upon our course. However, we reached our destination just as the sun was going down. Brabies had no rock-saucer; its water was held in a vley, or shallow depression with a hard clay bottom. This vley was several hundred yards in circumference. It lay on an almost imperceptible rise; nevertheless this circumstance enabled anyone camping on its margin to gain a view over an immense area of desert. Usually, we had been told, at least one heavy thunderstorm broke over Brabies early in each season, and then the vley held water for about three weeks.

With the exception of a few small troops of ostriches, immensely far off, no game was in sight. However, a long, low ridge—rising so slightly above the general level that the eye had difficulty in recognising it as an elevation at all—lay to the northward, some six miles away. We knew that the tract just on the other side of that ridge was one of the favourite feeding-grounds of the oryx. And it was oryx and nothing else that we were just then interested in. Judging by the amount of spoor, some of it quite fresh, our game could not be very far off.

This more or less central area of Bushmanland,—a tract from ten to twelve hundred square miles in extent—was practically the last refuge of the oryx south of the Orange River. It is almost absolutely flat,—except on its northern and eastern margins, where the dunes intrude for an inconsiderable distance over its bounds. The tract is quite arid, but occasionally, in perhaps half-a-dozen spots, the underground rock-saucers hold water for from three to five weeks. So far as I had been able to ascertain, Brabies and one other, but nameless, vley were the only places in the whole enormous northern section of the desert where water ever lay on the surface. Brabies, as has been stated, usually contained water once, at least, during each season, but the other vley sometimes remained dry for years at a stretch. As might be imagined, the region was of no economic value.

Owing to the circumstance that a measure of informal police protection had been afforded to the vicinity of Brabies during the previous two years, practically all the oryx in the desert had there congregated. I estimated their number at about twelve hundred. There was no reason why those animals should not have increased and multiplied. Andries was a Field Cornet,—an office combining the functions of a constable with those of a justice of the peace. I had appointed him Warden of the Desert Marches and Chief Protector of the Oryx and the Ostrich. Between us, we managed to protect these animals more or less effectively. But—"thou shalt not muzzle the ox that treadeth out the corn."

The oryx evinces several interesting peculiarities. I have mentioned in a previous chapter the remarkable formation of its foot,—the membrane connecting the wide-spreading toes, which enables it to gallop scathless over the Kanya stones which cripple all other animals. Another abnormality is shewn in the way the hair lies. If one wished to stroke the back of an oryx one would have to do so from back to front, as the hair slopes in a reverse direction as compared with all other antelopes. The oryx fawn is born with horns about four inches long, but the points are capped with a plug-like mass of horny substance. This falls off when the animal is about three weeks old.

An oryx fawn, until it has reached the age of from three to four months, is a most extraordinary object. Its neck, chest and flanks are covered with long hair, vivid red in hue. It has a shaggy red mane and a big, black, muzzle; its ears are of enormous size. The first time I saw these creatures I almost mistook them for lions. Three of them stood up suddenly at a distance of about sixty yards and gazed at me. My horse was terrified to such an extent that he became unmanageable. It was only with difficulty that Andries was able to persuade me as to the true nature of the animals.

The male and female oryx are identical in the matter of marking and are of approximately the same height, but the male is the heavier in build. The horns of the female are longer and straighter than those of the male, but are not so thick.

Occasionally, in the cool season of the year, one used dogs in hunting the oryx. But unless a dog had been specially trained to the business, it was speedily killed. Under ordinary circumstances a dog most effectively attacks an animal behind or on the flank, but the oryx, without breaking his stride, can give a lightning-quick sweep with his formidable horns and impale anything within four feet of his heels or on either side. The dog that knows its business runs in front of the oryx, for the latter cannot depress his head sufficiently forward to make the horns effective against anything before it which is low on the ground. A trained dog can thus easily bring an oryx to bay, and hold him engaged until the hunter comes to close quarters.

Here may be noted a contrast between the habits of the larger desert antelopes and of those antelopes which live in the forest. In the desert it is the males which head the flight, leaving the females and the weaklings to fend for themselves. But in the forest the male covers the retreat of his family and is always the last to flee. There is probably some connexion between the foregoing rule and the circumstance that the female of the antelope of the desert,—the oryx, the hartebeest and the blesbuck—is horned more or less as the male is, whereas the females of the forest dwellers,—the bushbuck, the koodoo and the impala—are hornless.

The horses had been watered, fed and picketed; we had eaten our supper and finished our pipes. I took my kaross and wandered away for a few hundred yards so as to be alone and undisturbed by snoring men or snorting horses. The only possible cause of anxiety was in respect of snakes. We killed a large yellow cobra just at dusk. The spoor of the cobra,—the hooded yellow death,—could be seen among the tussocks in every direction. The previous year one of my men had had a horse killed by a snake close to where the wagon then stood; the skeleton of the animal was still in evidence.

In the vicinity of the Brabies vley the sand was rather firmer than in most other parts of the desert; consequently cities of the desert mice abounded. Where mice were plentiful, so were snakes; they seemed to live together underground on the best of terms. In summer it was only at night that the snakes emerged and wandered abroad. However, cobras or no cobras, I intended to camp by myself.

And then—once more the unutterable peace, the sumptuous palace of the night,—the purple curtains of infinity excluding all that made for discord,—the music of the whispering tongues that filled the void. How the limitless, made manifest in the throbbing universe of stars, responds to the infinite which the most insignificant human soul contains. These are the transcendent wonders which the mighty Kant bracketed together.

An utterance of Shakespeare—embodying one of those cosmic imaginings only he or Goethe could have expressed, came to my mind—"the prophetic soul of the wide world dreaming on things to come." If there be a spirit proper to our globe—a thinking and informing spirit—surely the desert should be its habitation. If such ever dwelt where men congregate, it does so no longer, for men have no longer leisure to think; they spend their strength in continuous futile labour, the fruits of which are ashes and dust. Leisure, opportunity to collate experience and appraise its results,—surely that is necessary to balanced thought,—towards being able to see things in their true proportions. But so-called progress has killed leisure.

Where, to-day, is the voice of Truth to be heard? Not in the frantic and contradictory shoutings of the forum or the market place, nor in the groans of those doomed to unrequited and unleisured toil,—but I think that an attentive ear may sometimes hear her voice whispering in the wilderness. And this I know: that when a spent and wounded soul steals out and sinks humbly at the feet of Solitude, some kind and bountiful hand holds out to it the cup of Peace,—and often the pearl of Wisdom is dissolved in that cup for the spirit's refreshment.

Chapter Ten.
The Oryx Hunt—Terrible Thirst—Prehistoric Weapons.

Soon after daybreak we saddled up. That day our hunting was to be northward, for thither all the oryx spoor trended. Andries, Hendrick and I rode off together. We had to pass the western end of the long, low ridge noted on the previous evening. Hendrick, just before we started, declared that he saw some "black sticks" protruding near the ridge's eastern extremity. This was difficult to credit when one took the distance into consideration, yet we could not help admitting that the Hun had never yet misled us. So we proceeded on the reasonable assumption that his eyes had not on this occasion played him false.

Assuming the oryx to be where Hendrick affirmed he had seen their horns, we had to endeavour to give the animals our wind from the proper distance. In hunting the oryx one has to follow a method opposite to that followed in the case of all other game. If one got their wind, failure was a foregone conclusion, for the oryx cannot run down the wind. To keep up the necessary supply of oxygenated blood to his mighty muscles he must run—his wide nostrils expanded like funnels—against the air-current. Should he attempt to run down the wind he would smother when hard pressed. This both he and the hunter know, so the great art in the noble sport of oryx-hunting lies in manoeuvring so as to prevent the game from taking the only course on which his powers will have full play.

The day promised to be hot; when the Kalihari wind blows in summer there is no possibility of cool weather in the desert. We advanced at a walking pace, for the strength of our horses had to be conserved against that long pursuit which, in hunting the oryx, is almost inevitable. The heat grew greater every moment. The morning was at seven; what would the sunshine be like at noon?

We reached the western limit of the ridge,—where the gentle slope merged itself almost imperceptibly into the plain. This was the juncture at which to exercise caution; one false move then, and our day would have been wasted. We dismounted and stole cautiously to our right—Hendrick and I,—Andries remaining with the horses. A low "s-s-s-t" from Hendrick, and we dropped in our tracks to the ground. The keen-eyed Hun had again discerned the tips of the "black sticks" over the rim of the earth-curve. We crept back to Andries and the horses, held a council of war and finally decided upon our strategy.

Andries was heavily built; almost corpulent. This to him was a matter of great grief. His mount was strong, but no horse that ever was foaled could, with sixteen stone on its back, run down a herd of oryx.

Hendrick and I, accordingly, were to do the riding. The game was still several miles away, on our left front as we turned and faced the camp, but it nevertheless was necessary that we should make another wide sweep so as to get further to windward. So we rode off northward, leaving Andries behind. He decided to remain where he was, it being an even chance as to whether the herd, after it had started, would break past him or to the north-eastward. In any event its course would not be more than 45 degrees on either side of the point from which the wind was blowing. Andries, moreover, had an almost uncanny knack of forecasting the movements of wild animals.

Hendrick and I had got to within about three miles of the herd, and well to windward, when it sighted us. It was a fairly large one,—numbering about eighty head. Until the oryx started running we would continue to ride diagonally away from them, edging slightly to our right and proceeding at a walking pace. But I kept my head turned far enough over my right shoulder to enable me to keep one careful eye on the herd, which stood at gaze, every head pointing northward against the wind.

Our plans had been carefully laid. When the herd started running, as it now soon would, Hendrick, on his fierce black stallion, was to ride due east at full gallop, so as to cut clean across its course. My own actions would be governed by the behaviour of the game. I was anxious, if possible, to secure Andries a shot. At length the herd started and Hendrick, tense with desire, loosened his reins and thundered away. The course of the flight was, as we expected, a little to the east of north. It is remarkable how experience teaches one to anticipate what game will do when disturbed. I edged to my right at a moderate canter. Old Prince tried to break into a gallop, but the time for that was not yet.

57

The herd inclined its course still more to the eastward, but Hendrick had too much of a start for that to matter; he had, so far, the hunt completely in hand. Should the oryx have adhered to the course they started on, they would soon have been in a dilemma: that of having to choose between passing Hendrick at close quarters and running down the wind. So the inevitable alteration in their course was now only a matter of seconds. Ha! they swerved; they were now heading for the opening between Andries, whom, being behind the end of the ridge, they could not see, and myself. This was precisely what we had been manoeuvring for.

I let Prince out and galloped towards the advancing herd, pressing it gently away from the wind. Were I to have pressed the oryx too hard, they would have again swerved to their right and rushed for the opening between Hendrick and me. This would have suited me, personally, well enough, but would have spoilt Andries' chance. On they came—the full-grown bulls, about thirty of them— leading in a close phalanx. Then came the cows; behind these the fawns. I trended slightly to my right and gave Prince a looser rein. I had the herd fully in hand at about five hundred yards; I was easily holding their wind and could have closed with them whenever I liked. But, disregarding Andries' oft-repeated advice, I yielded to temptation. After gaining another hundred yards I rolled from my horse and opened fire. It seemed impossible to miss such a mark, but my first wind had gone and the second had not yet taken its place. My bullets went all over the veld, every shot missed.

As I remounted, with shame and sorrow in my heart, I heard a shot from the other side of the herd; it was followed by a thud. Then a bull turned out of the press; it faltered, staggered and fell. Once more I let Prince out at his best gallop, keeping his nose on the flank of the phalanx. I had, through my foolish impatience, largely lost my advantage; now my only chance of a favourable shot was to ride for all I was worth, strenuously pressing the leaders of the herd away from the wind.

The herd was then about nine hundred yards away. All I could do was to continue the pressure, so as to defer the now inevitable stern chase for as long as possible. I was just barely holding my own, but that was good enough for the current stage. The oryx did not as yet venture to turn up wind; they well knew that an attempt to do so would have enabled me to close with them by putting on a spurt.

Prince knew his work and had settled down to that steady, tireless stride I knew and loved so well, and which he could easily keep up for ten miles without a rest. The wind sang as we cleft it, rushing through the swaying "toa." The desert lay before us as level as the sea. A few springbucks, waifs from some trekking herd, stood at gaze as we swept by. They knew quite well what my objective was and accordingly were not alarmed. Paauws arose here and there on heavy wings; the flight of one startled all others in sight. Ostriches scudded away in various directions. The desert was awake; word of the presence of man,—of the arch-enemy on the war-path—had been borne to its farthest bounds.

The course of the herd was a segment of the periphery of a wide circle; my course was also a curve, but an elliptical one,—for it continually impinged on the leaders so as to continue pressing them away from the wind for every possible yard. But it was clear that very soon the oryx would be able to attain the course which was the object of their swift endeavour; this was rendered inevitable from the moment of my stupid blunder in dismounting too soon and thus throwing away my rare advantage. At length they had it; I could press them no longer. Now the flight is almost dead against the wind; now the trumpet-like nostrils are opened wide against the streaming current of air. This seems to stimulate the fugitives, for the distance between us has perceptibly increased.

Prince, unbidden, swerved to the right course and we followed hard on the heels of the flying game. It was at length a stern chase. A word to my faithful horse and his stride quickened. Soon it was clear that we were gaining. Herein was an illustration of how the instinct of animals, usually so true, may occasionally mislead them. These creatures, in the hour of danger blindly surrendering to the gregarious idea ingrained through the experience of ages, crowded so hard on each other that they got half-smothered in their own dust. Hence it is far more easy to ride down a large herd of oryx than a small one. When it is a case of a single animal, or even of two or three, a stern chase is almost hopeless, no matter how swift one's mount.

I was gaining rapidly; I overhauled the fawns and immature animals and pressed through, passing some of them within a few yards. One I had to turn out of my way by leaning forward from the saddle and prodding it with the muzzle of my rifle. Those young things followed after me, bent only on overtaking their elders; apparently oblivious of the circumstance that I was their enemy. I overtook the crowd of cows; it opened out and scattered on either hand. I was now riding in a cloud of dust, the phalanx of bulls being only about a hundred and fifty yards ahead; the animals could be but dimly discerned through the dust-cloud. I had to gain another hundred yards without attempting to dismount; not again would I yield to impatience.

The hundred yards were soon gained; Prince shewed signs of flagging, so I had to look out for a soft place whereon I could roll from the saddle without hurting myself. My second wind had come; I was as steady as a rock, but eyes, throat and nostrils were smarting from the acrid, pungent dust. I dropped the reins on Prince's neck; he shortened his stride and I rolled from his back on my right-hand side. I could just see the bulls, but the dust was so thick that it was impossible to pick an animal, so I fired into the brown of the moving mass. My bullet thudded hard; that was enough,—I would not fire again.

The herd of oryx sped on; I remounted and followed at a slow canter. Yes,— there was my quarry,—a bull turned out of the press and faltered in his course. I rode towards him; he still cantered but his gait was laboured. He stood, turned and faced me.

He was a noble brute,—a leader among the oryx people. Still as a statue he stood, defying his enemy. His wire-like hair was erect and quivering; his red, trumpet-formed nostrils seemed to exude defiance; his shoulders and flanks were heavily banded with streaks of foam. In spite of the long chase he did not appear to pant.

I dismounted when within about sixty yards and advanced towards the doomed and stricken creature. Now it behoved me to be wary, for had the bull charged and my shot failed to disable him, my death would inevitably have resulted. So I took careful aim at a spot just above where his neck emerged from his chest, and fired. The bull sank to the ground in a huddled heap.

I now became aware for the first time that I was suffering from raging thirst. To my dismay I found that the small flask of weak whiskey and water I had slung to the side of my saddle had got smashed in the course of the gallop. Away—in the far distance—I saw Hendrick approaching at a walk.

I disembowelled the oryx and covered the carcase with bushes so as to conceal it from the vultures. Among the bushes I burnt a few charges of gunpowder; this would serve to keep off the jackals—at all events for a few hours. Then I mounted and rode slowly towards the wagon. Hendrick altered his course and joined me, en route. Black Bucephalus looked piebald as he approached, so flaked was he with dried sweat.

The wagon was about twelve miles from where the oryx had fallen. It took us over three hours—hours of intense physical anguish—to travel those miles. My mouth was so parched that the saliva had ceased to exude, my lips were cracked and bleeding. For a considerable portion of the time spent on that dolorous journey I was on the verge of delirium. Hendrick also suffered, but in a somewhat less degree, for his fibre was tougher than mine. When about half-way to the wagon he asked my permission to ride apart, stating as his reason that he could not bear the sight of my torment. Brabies and the white tilt of the wagon seemed to recede before us. I then realised clearly how people might die on the threshold of relief. For untold gold I would not undergo another such experience.

But the journey came to an end at length, and the long drink which followed was unspeakably delicious. Soon the wagon was emptied of its contents and, with a team of eight fresh horses, despatched to fetch in the game. It was nightfall when the wagon returned with its heavy load,—the carcases of two large oryx bulls.

The morrow we spent at Brabies for the purpose of giving the horses a rest. We occupied ourselves in the prosaic process of cutting up and salting the oryx meat. On the following day we would start for home. The water of the vley was rapidly drying up under the fierce heat; in another week there would not be a drop left.

There were several features of interest connected with the vley. The water had shrunk to a series of small puddles. Swimming about in every one of these were large numbers of tiny organisms, each with a single, immense eye. These creatures belonged to a species of "Apus,"—a genus of one of the crustacean sub-families. On a trip undertaken during the previous year I had found an Apus of another species in a vley less than thirty miles from Brabies,—a vley which probably does not contain water more than once in five years. This development of separate species in localities so close to each other, suggested that local conditions had not materially changed for a very long period. No vley was found to contain more than a single variety. These quaint creatures swim through their little hour of fully developed life and, when the drying up of the water kills them, the eggs they contain are freed. Then these are blown hither and thither among the dust of the desert until another adventitious shower fills the vley in which they were generated, and some chance wind-gust carries a few of them into the water. The indefinite preservation of the life-germ on the occasionally almost red-hot surface of the desert is little short of miraculous.

Yes,—the Brabies vley must have existed under approximately similar conditions from an immensely remote antiquity. It is probable that in comparatively recent times rain was more plentiful in Bushmanland (as there is reason to believe it was generally throughout South Africa), than it now is. For there were evidences that Brabies was once a centre of population. Pottery, obviously of Bushman manufacture, abounded. If one broke a fragment, the charred fibres of the woven grass-blades on which the clay design had been formed, could be clearly seen. In the low, stone ledges surrounding the vley were to be seen grooves evidently caused by the sharpening of weapons. Some of these grooves were very deep, and as the Bushmen's arrow-heads were made of bone, the scores must have been the result of sharpening by many generations. A few of them looked as fresh as if they had been used the previous day.

A careful search discovered stone implements of various types,—palaeolithic as well as neolithic. These suggested a receding succession of prehistoric peoples to days unthinkably remote. Some of the weapons were very peculiar,— they were either spear-heads or arrow-heads. But they seemed too small for the former and too large for the latter. If they were spear-heads they must have been used by pygmies; if arrow-heads by giants.

As there were apparently no springbucks worth the hunting on that side of the desert, we decided to return home at once. We thus had no opportunity of testing the qualities of the fearsome hunting-chariot-contraption constructed by Andries. I was not altogether sorry; my bones ached in anticipation of our probable experiences in it,—behind the half-broken team.

Each morning when the sun first grew hot, the vley was invaded by countless myriads of desert grouse. Of these we shot some hundreds, which we salted down for home consumption.

Chapter Eleven.

The Richtersveld—Kuboos—The Vicar of Wakefield Redivivus—Gold-Seeking—The Raad—Morbid Sensibility—Start for El Dorado.

Just before the Orange River, wearied from its long travail, slides into the Atlantic, it bends in a sickle-shaped curve. Its course for the previous three hundred miles has been through the tremendous and almost inaccessible gorge into whose depths it hurled itself at the Augrabies Falls.

The incidence of those aggregates of men which pass, like the individual, through the successive stages of youth, maturity and decay, and which we are accustomed to term civilisations, is as much a question of geology as of geography. Accadia and Egypt grew great and stained many pages of the record we term history by virtue of the circumstance that the Euphrates and the Nile, after leaving the mountains that gave them birth, flowed respectively through low, level countries which they enriched with precious alluvium. The Orange River was, however, sped oceanwards over a vast plateau of hard-grained rock, several thousand feet above sea-level. Into this the stream has been slowly biting, and the alluvium—that meat upon which material civilisation is nourished, was hurled through the channel and flung wastefully into the maw of the all-consuming waves. Under different physiographical circumstances another Alexandria might have arisen where to-day the flamingo nests among the misty dunes at the Orange River's mouth, "and another Sphinx, of Hottentot or Bantu physiognomy, might have stood, gazing through forgotten centuries, across the waste of Bushmanland." (*Between Sun and Sand.*)

ORYX RESTING AT NOONDAY

The tract lying within the sickle-bend is called the Richtersveld. Little is known of this tract or of its inhabitants. Half a century ago prospecting for copper ore was carried on in the vicinity. Indications of the metal abounded, but no payable deposit was discovered.

I decided to organise an expedition to the Richtersveld. There were several reasons for doing this. One was a complaint which had been made to the Attorney General of the Cape Colony respecting the alleged flogging of a man under orders of the missionary at Kuboos, which is still haunted by the ghost of an institution established by the London Missionary Society in years long gone by. Another was a reported discovery of gold. This, as a matter of fact was my ostensible excuse for starting at the time I did. Third and last was my own keen desire to explore a little-known tract and make the acquaintance of its human and other inhabitants.

The Richtersveld, according to report, was extremely mountainous and was said to contain only some two hundred people of Koranna-Bushman and Hottentot descent. So remote and isolated was this region that its dwellers were tacitly permitted to govern themselves. They had a "raad" or council of elders which, under presidency of the missionary, settled all disputes and generally administered justice,—informal, but none the less just on that account. The language spoken by the Richtersvelders is an almost extinct Hottentot dialect, full of clicks, gutterals and phonetic excursions impossible to the average European tongue. Only a few of the people had even the merest smattering of Dutch.

That excursion involved more difficulties than any other I had undertaken. There was, it is true, not more than a bare hundred miles of desert to cross, but the only definite information we had been able to gain as to the route was to the effect that it led through a tract practically waterless and extremely difficult to traverse. Moreover, it was reported to be absolutely uninhabited. One thing was quite clear,—we should have to travel with oxen; horses would have been useless under the conditions as described.

Andries arrived bringing—not the comfortable, tilted, spring-wagon,—but the strong, heavy, tentless "buck" wagon, with a team of sixteen picked oxen. He seemed uneasy as to our prospects, for the coast desert had a bad reputation and we were about to plunge into a wilderness with the conditions of which he was unfamiliar. The map was produced, but Andries rather despises maps. This one shewed little beyond "gaps" and "unhabitable downs." But it indicated, roughly, our obvious route. We would travel alongside the copper-trolley-line as far as Anenous, which lay at the foot of the mountain range and thus on the inner margin of the coast desert,—which is little, if at all, above the level of the sea. From Anenous we had to trend to the north-west, past Tarabies, Lekkersing and the northern trigonometrical beacon. Thence via Hell Gate to Kuboos, where the wagon would have to remain. Any further journeyings would apparently have to be undertaken on foot. Possibly, however, we might be able to obtain pack-oxen.

Judging by the map, the course looked obvious and easy, but we knew that the surface of the coast desert was composed of deep, soft sand, into which the wheels of the heavy wagon would sink deeply, and that through the sandy tract the northern range of mountains sent out spines or dykes of rock, many miles in length. These, we were told, often took the form of abrupt ridges extremely difficult to negotiate with any vehicle, no matter how strongly built.

The officials of the Cape Copper Company at Anenous (which was the jumping-off place for our hundred-mile sand-swim) knew nothing of the country two miles on either side of the trolley-line. All they were definite about was that no one had ever been known to arrive at Anenous from the northward or north-westward.

Such Hottentots as we were able to consult all declared that it was only under very exceptional circumstances that water was to be found between the trolley-line and the Orange River.

Andries' feelings must have resembled those of a seaman ordered to navigate his ship through an uncharted archipelago. Owing to our absolute lack of local knowledge we should be constrained to do all our travelling by day, and this meant severe suffering for the cattle. In the old days of prospecting for copper ore, all communication with the Richtersveld was effected by a route along the actual sea-shore from Port Nolloth to the Orange River's mouth and thence inland along the river bank to the sickle-bend.

We started from Anenous very early in the morning. On the previous day we had kept the oxen without water, so that almost to the moment of commencing the journey they might be very thirsty, and accordingly drink their fill. We at once plunged into the waste of sand; this proved to be so heavy that we were unable to travel at a higher rate than two miles an hour. The country was quite different from the Bushmanland plains; there was no "toa," but succulent plants of great variety were plentiful. One Mesembryanthemum had the dimensions of a large cabbage. In spite of its succulence the oxen would not eat of this vegetation.

The climate, also, was different from that of the Bushmanland plains; the heat was not so great, but what there was of it proved exhausting. A haze brooded over the earth; through it the north-western mountain range loomed gigantic and mysterious. There were no roads,—unless a wide-meshed network of half-obliterated tracks—probably old game-paths—could be described as such. One strange peculiarity of the coastal desert is the extraordinary persistence of spoor and other markings on the surface of the ground. Near Walfish Bay the clear tracks of elephants may still be seen,—and there has not been an elephant in the vicinity for upwards of half a century.

After desperate efforts we reached Kuboos on the afternoon of the fourth day. I never thought it possible that a wagon could travel where ours did. We ploughed through calamitous expanses of sand, we floundered through dusty dongas. We bumped and clattered over high, steep-sided ramparts of rock. But the skill of Andries as a driver, the endurance of the oxen and the strength of the wagon brought us safely through.

The quaint little collection of ramshackle buildings forming the missing station, was perched on a ledge just below where the more or less gradual descent of the T'Oums Mountain falls steeply into the gorge, at the bottom of which the dry bed of the Anys River lies. In the centre stood, skeleton-like, the inevitable unfinished church, its narrow gables uplifted like clamorous hands to heaven in an apparently vain appeal for funds.

The groaning, bumping wagon came to a halt before a low cottage built of sun-dried bricks and thatched with reeds. From it emerged a figure startling in its incongruity. This was a tall, elderly, erect man dressed in black broad-cloth, with a bell-topper and a very voluminous white choker. He was coloured; that was quite evident, but the stately dignity of his stride as he advanced, and the courtly grace of his demeanour when he greeted us, could not have been improved upon by a Chesterfield. Self-confidence and a complete ease of manner were apparent in every word, in every graceful gesture. He spoke in High Dutch, before which my homely "taal" faltered, abashed. I should say his age was nearer seventy than sixty. This was the Reverend Mr Hein, Resident Missionary of Kuboos and Dictator of the Richtersveld.

Feeling somewhat subdued, we followed Mr Hein to his dwelling, where he ushered us through the lowly portal. The room we entered was small and poorly furnished, but scrupulously clean. The thong-bottomed sofa and chairs were evidently home-made; although rough in point of workmanship they were strong and comfortable. The walls were garnished with illuminated Bible texts and portraits of the Royal Family. The floor was of clay; the thatch of the roof could be seen through a gridiron of rafters.

Mr Hein took the head of the table and played the host to perfection. We had evidently been expected,—but how information as to our projected visit could have reached Kuboos, was more than I could fathom. However, we sat at the hospitable board and regaled ourselves with excellent coffee, rye bread and honey. The members of the family,—two fairly young men and two middle-aged damsels,—joined us. Mrs Hein was, alas, no more. She had died under a weight of years, so we were informed, a few months previously. The sons and daughters were darker in hue than their father. They were obviously ill at ease before us, strangers.

The host kept the conversational ball rolling without an effort. Andries was pathetically puzzled; the situation had got beyond him. He was as prejudiced on the Colour Question as are most colonists; in the abstract he hated the idea of sitting at table with coloured people. But on this occasion he felt himself to be completely outclassed in the items of manners and culture; consequently he became acutely embarrassed. However, he appreciated the coffee (he told me afterwards that his own wife, who had a wide reputation as a coffee-maker, could not have made it better) and the bread and honey were delicious.

Of whom was it that Mr Hein reminded me? His personality set some familiar chord vibrating. Was it—yes, it was—Parson Primrose; it was he and none other. I tried to extend the parallel. Either of the sons might, at a pitch, have passed for Moses. George? Well,—hardly. Olivia and Sophia?—Oh, well—hm—that was another matter. But at all events there was the dear old Vicar, reincarnated under a yellow skin, in that citadel of loneliness that had a hundred-mile fosse of desert sand and a rampart of all-but-impassible mountains,—that most remote corner of the habitable world. Chamisso was right:—

"Alle menschen sind einander gleich."

Next morning I met the "Raad," and we discussed the matter of the flogging. That Raad was a quaint assemblage; surely the most peculiar parliament on earth. It was composed of elderly men, all of a more or less monkeylike physiognomy. Mr Hein took the chair and filled it with the utmost dignity. The members were restrained in manner, temperate in discussion and logical in all they said. Their delivery was pleasing, the rules of debate were strictly observed. Several of the speeches were made in Dutch; those given in the Hottentot tongue were interpreted into Dutch for my benefit.

The individual who had received the flogging was present. He was a young married man with a weak chin, a shifty eye and a voluble tongue. His face possessed a certain measure of meretricious good-looks, evidently he was a lady-killer; one of the cheaper varieties of that species. He, an officer of the church, had committed an offence against the moral law. The partner in his guilt was present, looking sufficiently woe-begone. She did not possess the fatal gift of beauty,—at all events according to Caucasian standards. The injured spouse, attired in a goatskin robe, was present and wept softly at intervals throughout the proceedings. She was distinctly less uncomely than the erring sister.

The Raad had dealt with the case and sentenced the culprit, who had admitted his guilt, to receive three dozen with a "strop," which were immediately and energetically inflicted. The punishment, although illegal, had been richly deserved. I considered that the Raad had acted with propriety,—but it was necessary to be guarded in what I said. If the principle involved had been given formal official sanction, it might have been logically applied to more serious cases,—those, for instance, in which capital punishment would have been due. If, at some future time, the Vicar under my implied authority had erected a gallows and engaged the services of a Lord High Executioner, it would have been awkward, to say the least of it.

Accordingly I temporised. Lothario of the shifty eye was informed that his case would be duly considered at head-quarters. So it would,—by the moths inhabiting the pigeonholes of the Record Office in Cape Town. Nevertheless I should have to deal cunningly with this episode so as to avoid raising a humanitarian howl. However, I meant, so far as I could to support the authority of the Raad. The result of discrediting that would have been to loosen the bonds of the moral law,—to hand the Richtersveld over to be exploited by the violent and lawless. This Raad interested me extremely; it was so wise and so conscientious. The Colonial Parliament might really have learnt quite a lot of useful things from it.

We are a curious people. The solicitude we are apt to evince for the posterior of a blackguard is really marvellous—considering how little we have for the victims of an industrial system under which hundreds of thousands of men, women and children are leading lives of the most degrading slavery. We see, with complacency, whole generations growing stunted and vacant-eyed under stress of their bitter lot; we know—or should know, for we have been told it often enough—that one of the pillars in the edifice of our commercial prosperity is the sweated woman in the garret,—old, haggard and hopeless at thirty. She stitches or pastes for fourteen hours a day in the blind, numbing effort to keep her blighted soul in her stunted body, and we complacently draw the dividends her long-drawn torture helps to swell. But we forget it is that woman's grandchildren who may have to defend ours from the Huns.

Yes,—a fatal habit of acquiescing in demoralising conditions permits us to look on at, without attempting to prevent, the slow, relentless murder of a race. But the blackguard's back—that is something sacred; the mere idea of its being defiled by the richly deserved lash fills us with horror. The divine force of indignation which is in the heart of every man,—a holy thing when used for the right purpose—is thus wasted, dissipated—fired off at a straw dummy held

66

aloft, as it were, by Commercialism for the purpose of drawing our attention from its own foul works.

And if we came to honestly examine our own feelings on the subject we should find that it was not so much the blackguard who was in question as our own morbid sensibility. We—that is the ones who live on the labour of others,—the small minority who, feasting on the deck of the ship of western civilisation which is being steered straight for the abyss—have sunk into what Schiller called "*der weichlichen Schoss der Verfeinerung*" our hyperaesthesia has grown so morbid that every stripe we see administered raises a weal on ourselves. This is a condition perilously near that in which the contemplation of suffering becomes the sole channel of pleasure, for morbid sensibility and cruelty have usually hobnobbed at the same inn. It is the healthy man who does not shrink from either enduring or inflicting necessary pain.

The Raad was dissolved—dismissed with my blessing which, however, I felt constrained to express in more or less guarded terms. I regarded that body with deep and sincere admiration. It might be of incalculable benefit to the British Empire if the speakers of the respective parliaments of the self-governing Colonies, led by the speaker of the House of Commons, were to visit the Richtersveld and sit on that arid hillside listening to the Raad's deliberations. I should be prepared personally to conduct the tour.

With the Vicar's kind assistance I proceeded with the necessary preparations for my gold-seeking adventure. He lent me some carpenter's tools, and I soon altered a small gin-case I had brought into a very fair imitation of a gold-digger's cradle. The next step was to hire two pack-oxen and secure the services of a few labourers. On the following morning we would start for the supposed El Dorado. In the meantime I again called on my interesting friend the Vicar, drank some more of his excellent coffee, and, after contributing according to my means towards the building fund of the unfinished church, bade my host a cordial farewell.

It was a quaint caravan which next morning scarped the north-eastern shoulder of the T'Oums Mountain, in search of El Dorado. The guide—a little, wizened creature, certainly more than half Bushman—and I, led the procession. Next came the pack-oxen, conducted by their respective owners, but generally under Hendrick's charge. The loads were miscellaneous in character, but not heavy. They comprised my bedding, provisions, delving tools and receptacles for such reptiles, insects and plants as we might find it worth while to collect. From the top of one load the handle of the cradle pointed towards heaven—or rather it would have had it not swayed so much from the gait of the ox. I wished for a small flag to attach to it. Next came a mixed crowd, about twenty in number. These were mere camp followers, but they insisted on accompanying me. They included men, women and children. Among the latter were two ape-like babies, slung on their mothers' backs. Andries, for the time, had remained behind with the wagon.

The track was unexpectedly good; much better in fact than the one over which we had travelled before reaching Kuboos. To the left, in the direction of the Orange River, the scenery was comparatively tame,—that is to say it looked as though one might pass over the country without inevitably breaking one's neck. But to the right lay chaos, confused and titanic. The strata were completely inverted—in some instances almost turned upside down. But the general suggestion was as though several miles of the earth's surface-crust had been placed on end. The soft layers had disappeared; the hard remained standing. Alternate deep chasms and jutting, mountainous buttresses of rock were the consequence.

That sickle-bend must have been the result of a tremendous cosmic upheaval—an earth-throe which flung aside like a wisp the from thirty to forty miles of double mountains bounding the then-steep river gorge. A good deal of the former surface of the bend had disappeared. Then the river, no longer a captive in adamant bonds (as it still is farther inland) doubtless took advantage of the unstable conditions brought about by the cataclysm, laid hands on the shattered earth-ribs and hurled them, piecemeal, from its path. So that there, although the mountains were even loftier than those farther to the eastward, they did not press upon the river as though trying to strangle it.

So far as I could make out El Dorado was about twenty miles from Kuboos. As we proceeded the track improved. The guide now calmly informed me that we had passed the worst of it. Therefore all the trouble and expense of hiring the pack-oxen and their owners was unnecessary. Here evaporated another illusion; these people had developed business instincts; the serpent of guile had found its way even to the Richtersveld paradise. I scribbled a note asking Andries to follow on our spoor with the wagon. This note I sent back by one of the camp followers.

It was fairly late in the afternoon when we reached our destination. The guide pointed out to me the exact spot where the nugget was alleged to have been picked up. It was on the side of a little gully which scarred the terraced bank of the dry T'Cuidabees River. The bedrock was of soft shale; it almost protruded from the surface, so sparse was the covering soil. There was no such thing as "wash" in the ordinary sense, but merely earth to the depth of a few inches, with which a good many angular quartz pebbles were mixed. I had once found gold, in an almost exactly similar formation, at a spot in the north-eastern Transvaal.

But how to test the ground; that was the question. My principal object in sending for the wagon was the conveyance of a few loads of gravel to the nearest water,—wherever that might be. In the meantime I set a party of my followers to work loosening the soil and picking out the stones. By the time darkness set in we had as much "wash" ready as we would be able to deal with.

The Trek-Boers used to say that rain always followed me to Bushmanland. It had apparently followed me to the Richtersveld, for as we sat at the camp fire a menacing black cloud climbed into and filled the northern sky over the mountains of Great Namaqualand; every few seconds it was illuminated by fantastic lightning explosions. As the cloud drew nearer the thunder began to speak. Soon a black fog rolled down on us and a veritable thunderstorm set in. For upwards of an hour the rain fell heavily. We got wet through, but I was much consoled in the discomfort by information from the Hottentots to the effect that there was a deep hole some few hundred yards down the river-course, which held water for several days after the rare occasions upon which rain fell. Soon the storm had passed away, so we built up a huge fire and got our clothes more or less dried. Then to sleep.

In the morning the cradle was conveyed down the valley to where the water was supposed to be. Sure enough, the hole was as described; we found it full to the brim of muddy water. Although only a few feet in width it was deep. Probably it held four hundred gallons. Work was started at once,—all my followers, male as well as female, carrying down the loosened gravel in their skin garments which, to my embarrassment, they discarded (as clothing) for the occasion. The cradle stood at the side of the pool, so that the water, after it had passed through the sieve and over the trays, could run back. One of the men lifted the water in a bucket and poured it slowly into the top of the cradle, while I rocked. After running through the equivalent of a few barrow-loads I removed the top tray and examined what lay behind the lip. Yes, veritably—there were a few tiny specks of gold.

This was what gold-diggers call "a pay prospect," for the gold was rough and not water-worn. It was quite evident that this gold had never been under the influence of water at all, but had lain *in situ* where the decomposing matrix had deposited it. I kept the cradle going until the water in the pool had the consistency of pea-soup; then I perforce stopped. The result was a nice little "prospect" of some seven or eight pennyweights. This was distinctly a payable proposition—or rather it would have been had permanent water existed in the vicinity.

Andries arrived with the wagon at about midday; he was much impressed by the find. Then we began an examination of the surrounding country, taking small quantities of "wash" here and there from likely-looking spots. These were sent back to the water-hole with instructions that the various lots were to be kept separate. When the liquid had cleared a little I recommended cradling. However, except in one instance, I did not find a single "colour." The exception was in respect of a parcel of "wash" taken from the margin of the dry bed of the river. This was found to contain a small speck,—one most likely washed down from the terrace where we had worked in the first instance. However, the existence of a practically payable gold-field in that vicinity was inconceivable, in view of the almost unmitigated aridity.

The country had the appearance of being highly mineralised; quartz reefs ran like white threads in every direction. Copper-carbonate stains were to be seen on many of the rock-ledges and I was able to trace a narrow vein of galena for a considerable distance. A systematic examination of the geological formation of that region would have been of great interest.

There was little or no animal life, and what little existed did not add to one's comfort. While the sun was shining existence was made a burthen by a blue fly which continually fed on one; it was about the size of a horse-fly. The bite, not felt at the time, was followed by a flow of blood and afterwards caused considerable irritation. We killed several poisonous snakes. The only antelopes we saw were klipspringers, but they were too far off to shoot, and our time was too limited to admit of our pursuing them.

Mr Hein had told me that there was a small troop of zebras to be found high up on the T'Oums Mountain. The mountain zebra is the wariest animal alive; it never lies down, but sleeps in a standing posture, with the muzzle resting on a stone.

I spent another day prospecting in the vicinity but could find no more gold. When, in the evening, we were sitting at the camp fire, an idea struck me. I then determined to take some food, a kaross, the guns and the collecting plant, and pay a flying visit to the area contained within the sickle-bend. With Hendrick and a couple of bearers I should be able to cover twenty miles a day. My plan was to strike north-east across the veld until I reached the river; then to follow, so far as possible, the course of the latter down to Arris, beyond Kuboos. Andries was to take the wagon back to Kuboos and thence to Arris, where he would wait for me. My journey, if I put my best foot forward, should not consume more than three days, and it would take Andries fully two by the more direct route.

I could but ill afford the time, but really all that was involved was the loss of one day. In all probability I should never have another opportunity of exploring the Richtersveld.

Andries grumbled at first, but eventually gave in. I reminded him that he might fill in his day of waiting by taking a walk from Arris to the mouth of the Orange River. An inspection of our stores shewed that we were still fairly well off. So Hendrick was sent to the scherms of our followers to call for volunteers—men who knew the country well—who would act as guides as well as carry our baggage.

My only regret was that I should lose the opportunity of bidding farewell to my excellent friend the Vicar.

Chapter Twelve.

Expedition to the River—Flora and Fauna—The Pneumoras— Abnormal Springbuck—The Sea-Fog—Wild Horses—Fauna and Bimini.

In the grey dawn I arose and resumed preparations for the expedition. When, after breakfast, I sent word to the scherms that I wished the guides to report themselves for duty, I was both flattered and embarrassed to find that every man, woman and child of my camp following was not only willing, but apparently determined to join my colours. The previous day had seen a considerable increase to the contingent, which now included two members of the Raad. The number was alarming; nearly twenty-five per cent, of the estimated population of the Richtersveld must have been in the vicinity of the camp. The fame of my liberality had gone forth; I had distributed some tobacco among the adults and with a few dates had gladdened the hearts of the children. But I could not afford to bestow largesse upon the crowd which at my call eagerly stood forth.

It was a strange gathering. The people reminded me of gnomes, so ugly were they—and their personal uncleanliness I fear corresponded with their looks. Yet I found them lovable, because they were natural, ingenuous and unspoilt. There was not a pair of breeches nor a petticoat among the lot; men and women were dressed either in brayed skins or ancient gunny-bags. The children were hardly dressed at all.

I think it was the feeling that I was honoured and appreciated far above my deserts by those people that caused me to like them so much. They looked upon me as a powerful and beneficent being of fabulous resources,—just because I had treated them with common fairness and given away a few pounds of cheap tobacco and some handfuls of dates.

One thing was clear: my influence was increasing; every hour fresh arrivals testified to the growth of my fame. I felt almost sure I could organise a successful revolution in the Richtersveld, attack Kuboos and sack it, depose Mr Hein, and reign in his stead. However, I at once put the temptation behind me. I had eaten the Vicar's honey and drunk his coffee; therefore, I would not rob him of his crown and kingdom. Besides,—who knew but that when my supply of tobacco and dates ran out, my popularity might not wane?

The immediate question as to who was to accompany me was a delicate one. Hendrick, of course, was chief of my staff. I only required two others, but ten— of whom four were women—clamoured insistently for enlistment, declaring that Hendrick had, the previous night, contracted with them individually and collectively for the intended trip. I explained the inadequacy of my reserve of food; I laid stress on the local scarcity of game. I was informed that at that time of year "veld-kost," the uncultivated produce of Nature's vegetable garden, was plentiful, and that monkeys abounded in the river forest. In despair I called up the two members of the Raad and begged of them to arbitrate. These men were diplomatists; they were accustomed to dealing with important questions.

A violent disputation followed; in the course of it the clicks of the Hottentot tongue flew about like fire-crackers. Eventually a most preposterous award was given. Five Richtersvelders—three men and two women—were to be enrolled as my corps of guides. One of the women was old; she might have passed for a revised edition of the Witch of Endor. However, she looked wiry. The other was young—not more than thirty. Was she married? Yes. Where was her husband? There he sat, with downcast visage, among the rejected. Then I would not take her. The lady was neither well-favoured nor savoury; nevertheless I had my character to consider, and the punishment locally prescribed for the abduction of a married woman—even with her husband's consent—might have been three dozen with a strop.

But the members of the Raad had selected her. She threw the tanned skin over her head and wailed. Beauty in distress prevailed; but her husband also had to be included in the contingent. The two ladies had names, but such were difficult to remember and almost impossible to pronounce, so I decided to substitute for them, respectively, Fauna and Flora. The special work of these insistent females was to be the collection of natural history specimens.

Very early that morning I sent some of the children out to look for reptiles, insects and miscellaneous small deer. It was principally beetles and lizards they brought back. None were very rare. *Julodis Gariepina*, a beetle somewhat resembling a green and yellow bottle-brush, I was glad to add to my stock for distribution. Of this there were a number of specimens. But one of the boys had brought three examples of an Orthopterous insect,—a *pneumora*, which was new to me. The *pneumora* is a large, green, bladder-like creature, whose whole body has been converted into a musical instrument; there is, in fact, a complete key-board on each flank. Using its trochanter as a plectrum, this insect makes weird music, which can be heard at a considerable distance. The youngster who had brought these quaint creatures received, in addition to the ordinary currency of dates, a special reward of three pence. The nearest shop where these could be spent was at Port Nolloth, upwards of a hundred miles away. This reckless liberality on my part was fraught with seriously embarrassing consequences. The *pneumora* is colloquially known as the "ghoonya."

At length we made a start. Andries was so amused at the details of my caravan that he almost became apoplectic. I felt sure that the regard my old friend had for me was often mitigated by doubts as to my sanity. The outlook of Andries was limited; however, he possessed the saving grace of a sense of humour.

Our course lay along the western side of the long, diminishing spur which almost connects the T'Oums range with the river, its compass-bearing being north-east by north. Fauna, the elder of the two ladies, was ordered to devote her attention to collecting zoological specimens. She was given a strong metal receptacle half filled with methylated spirits in which corrosive sublimate had been dissolved. In this she had to souse her trove of lizards, scorpions, centipedes and such snakes as were not too large. She also carried a cyanide bottle in which to immolate beetles and other insects. Flora was entrusted with a portfolio and directed to gather botanical specimens. She wandered far afield, gleaning the arid pastures. Fauna begged hard for permission to accompany her, but this I sternly refused. I was positive that—in spite of my solemn warnings on the subject—as soon as these women had got out of sight they would have drunk the poisoned spirit. If this had happened, the Raad might have hanged me. I realised what a dangerous precedent I had established in tacitly approving of the punishment inflicted on Lothario. Whilst Fauna carried that tank, she should not stir from my side.

We passed over some broken country and then reached a more or less level plateau, which seemed to extend almost to the river. Anon we crossed the ancient bed of what had once been a tributary river. It was as dry as the Bone-Valley of Ezekiel. Yet undoubtedly water had flowed therein, continuously, and that not so very long before. The course was full of deep, water-rounded drift. It was this kind of thing that brought home to one the circumstance that a great change in the direction of aridity must have taken place in South Africa within a comparatively short period. It was clear that not long previously this valley had carried a constantly-flowing stream,—one that took its source from the great T'Oums range. The latter, not more than ten miles away, was now arid as a heap of cinders.

As we approached the river the naked and enormous ramparts of the Great Namaqualand Mountains came more and more into evidence. They seemed to spring sheer from the narrow strip of forest at the water side. From a distance the upper strata appeared to be of black basalt. The purple mystery which so richly filled their vast chasms was a feast to the eye.

In the middle of the afternoon we reached the river. It was at half-flood. In the mass, the water looked muddy, but one could see the bottom of a pannikin filled with it, and the taste was delicious. The lovely, dark-green fringe of forest—generally continuous on both sides, but occasionally adorning one only—was soothing to gaze on. We rested for a while, and then took our course along the left-hand curve of the sickle-bend,—thus trending more to the north-westward. The way was extremely rough. When it was practicable to keep close to the river bank we made good progress, but now and then were obliged to recede for the purpose of avoiding rocky bluffs. Then our experiences were purgatorial, for we had to plunge into and climb out of a succession of deep, sand-choked clefts. On the southern bank of the river there was comparatively little forest.

Just about sundown we reached a wide terrace of stone below a cliff, and close to the water's edge, so we decided to camp there for the night. The only game we had seen was a covey of pheasants; of these I managed to bag three. I also shot two monkeys in the forest. I felt like a murderer in consequence,—but my followers had to be fed. They had had little or no opportunity of gathering "veld-kost."

I examined the collections of Flora and Fauna and carefully took possession of the tank of poisoned spirit. The spoil did not amount to very much. The most interesting item was a locust—very like those which occasionally over-run the Cape Colony, and do such enormous damage. It was, however, clearly a separate species, being larger and lighter in colour than the much-dreaded migratory insect.

Soon after we halted three boys approached along our trail, each carrying something with great care. They drew near, and with an air of conscious virtue, deposited their offerings at my feet.

One had brought a small, elongated, circular basket made of rushes, with the top carefully closed. I opened this and found it full of green, bladdery ghoonyas. There were dozens and dozens of them, squirming and crawling over one another. The next boy carried a rusty, battered nail-keg. This, likewise, contained ghoonyas. The third boy had denuded himself of his goatskin and tied a bunch in it, big enough to hold a moderate plum-pudding. This, too, was full of ghoonyas—green and bladdery, alive and squirming. The situation had got beyond me; words could not express my over-wrought feelings.

The *pneumoras*—several hundred of them—impatient after their long confinement and irritated at having been shaken about on the journey, climbed out of their respective prisons and began crawling about over the face of the rock, endeavouring to escape. The three boys, aided by Flora and Fauna, shepherded them back with twigs plucked for the occasion. I searched the remotest fastnesses of memory for a precedent to guide me, but could find none. Hendrick and the others looked on gravely. Had anyone laughed, murder would most likely have been committed. By my direction the shepherding operations were suspended and the ghoonyas fully restored to liberty.

73

Obviously, something had to be done. So as soon as my feelings were sufficiently under control I called up the interpreter and made a speech. I declared with emphasis that I did not want these ghoonyas; that I had been anxious to secure only a few specimens—half-a-dozen at most, but that I really and truly did not require or desire any more. However (and here is where I made a blunder) as that lot of insects had been collected on my behalf in good faith, I would reward the collectors to the extent of three pence each, plus a few dates. The gifts were joyfully accepted and the boys departed.

My enjoyment of the evening was largely spoilt by tarantulas. Hundreds of these, attracted by the light of the fire, came out from among the rocks and ran fearlessly among us. However, I managed to relish my supper of roast pheasant; while my followers indulged in a semi-cannibalistic repast of barbecued monkey. Then I lit my pipe, took my kaross and sought for a suitable couch some distance away. After lying down I felt something crawling on my neck; I sprang up, imagining it to be a tarantula, but it turned out to be only a ghoonya.

Dawn broke deliciously. The chanting falcons swooped from their cliff-eyries, and filled the morning with wild music. A swim in the swirling current would be a joy. I gave Hendrick my clothes in a bundle and sent him with them along the bank to a rocky point about a quarter of a mile down stream. I entered the water, swimming carefully while near the bank, for fear of snags. The current carried me luxuriously away. I emerged at the spot where my clothes were, and returned to camp for breakfast. All hands were foraging for "veld-kost" among the kopjes. Soon they returned, laden with strange vegetable spoil.

The previous day had been unusually cool, but that morning opened with a breath from the Kalihari,—the definite and unalterable promise of severe heat. This would last until the sea-breeze reached us, late in the afternoon. We marched along the river bank, admiring the towering bluffs that glowed in the sunshine and then allowing our eyes to sink down and drink refreshment from the delicious greenery of the forest. We were now well round the eastern section of the bend, and were travelling almost due west. More pheasants and monkeys fell to my gun. An army on the march must levy tribute on the territory it passes through.

The character of the country somewhat changed as the river curved southward. On the northern side of the river the mountains were not quite so high; on the southern, they now sprang steeply from the river bed. Here and there, under the overhanging edges of the higher terraces, we noticed caves. A murmur stole up the gorge and waxed as we advanced. It came from the steep and tortuous foaming rapids where the mighty chasm remade itself for a space. Here the river was as though flung like a ringlet among the menacing ranges.

But in view of the fact that we had not been able to make quite as much headway as I had anticipated, I regretfully felt constrained to leave the vicinity of the river for a time and take a course across some very rough country behind the south-western bluffs. We could not get from the guides an assurance of being able to make our way down through the tortuous gorge.

We soon reached a large, broken plateau, on which several small flocks of goats were grazing. Later, we found some scherms occupied by human beings. These rudimentary dwellings consisted of a few bushes piled, crescent-wise, against the wind. A rush mat, its position being altered with the changing hours, afforded shelter from the sun. Rain falls so seldom that it is not taken into account in the architecture of the Richtersveld. The dwellers in these scherms were of the same ill-favoured type as my guides. They were filled with curiosity as to the object of my expedition. But curiosity paled in the joy of receiving a little tobacco. And I found I could still spare a few dates for the children.

In one of the scherms was a newly-born baby, a girl. It weirdly resembled a hairless, light-yellow monkey. I made the mother very happy by presenting her with a shilling and my only pocket-handkerchief,—a red bandana. The shilling judiciously invested at compound interest, might provide the youngster with a dowry.

After a long, monotonous and extremely hot walk, we got beyond the convoluted gorge and once more began to descend towards the river. We now had a view of the level coast desert—or would have had if the landscape had not been to a great extent shrouded in fog. The river had widened and apparently become deeper. After its plunge into the abyss at Aughrabies, its struggle for many hundred miles through the depths of the black, torrid gorge,—it advanced with silent, stately, deliberate stride to rejoin the ocean—the mother that gave it birth.

The landscape ahead had completely altered its character. On the northern side of the river it was still mountainous, but the mountains had receded somewhat, and they rapidly decreased in height to the westward. On the southern side the mountain range came to an abrupt ending. Rounded hillocks emerged here and there from the plain which, as it approached the coast, was carpeted with patches of white, slowly-drifting fog. This made the detail difficult to appraise.

We descended the flank of the last really high mountain, intending to rest just below the lordly gate of the immense labyrinth from which we had emerged,—from the threshold of which the mist-shrouded plains extend to the Atlantic. For when the hot winds of the desert stream over the cold antarctic current that washes this coast, they draw up moisture which is blown back landward in the form of vapour. Herein lies the explanation of the circumstance that the coast desert is occasionally, for months at a time, densely shrouded in mist.

There—before the mountain gate—where the wearied water glided away in thankful silence from the last of the thunderous rapids that vexed its course,—was one of the favourite resorts of the only remaining school of sea-cows on that side of Africa, south of the tropical line. Of all the myriad hosts of wonderful wild creatures that until lately populated these desert plains and mountains, only this one school of hippopotami and a few hundred springbuck survive. I could hardly hope to find the sea-cows—at all events while daylight lasted; it would suffice if at night I might listen to their snorting and blowing—to the rustling in the reed-brakes as the huge creatures emerged from the water in search of food. These sounds would bring back memories of days long past—of adventures in other pastures of South Africa's rich and varied wonderland.

Before the sun had set we camped in a sandy hollow, a few hundred yards from the river's bank. There were no rocks in the immediate vicinity so we hoped to escape the usual plague of tarantulas. After a long, luxurious swim in the placid river, I returned to examine the collections of Flora and Fauna. The latter had been permitted to wander afield that day. The number of centipedes, scorpions and miscellaneous reptiles which had been soused in the poisoned spirit was so great that I no longer feared her attempting to sample it as a beverage. The harvest was more rich and interesting than usual. Flora had found a gorgeous stapelia with a more than ordinarily atrocious smell, and Fauna had captured a beetle infested with a most extraordinary parasite; also a small, speckled toad—a novelty, I thought—and a scorpion which, when stretched out, measured eight and a half inches. Well done, Fauna!

Hendrick had roasted a pheasant to a turn. I was savagely hungry; just as I was about to begin eating I noticed some people approaching along our trail. These comprised a man, two women and several children. I was filled with foreboding. The strangers approached, each carrying something with carefulness. They set offerings before me. These consisted of ghoonyas, and nothing else.

What did these people take me for; did they suppose I lived on a ghoonya diet—that I fed my caravan on ghoonya soup? Was I to have the extinction of an innocent species of orthoptera on my already burthened conscience; or would the result of all this be the adoption of the ghoonya as the totem of the Richtersveld Tribe? Those unlucky threepenny pieces,—my unfortunate enthusiasm over the first specimens—these seemed to have set the whole of the local population on the hunting trail for ghoonyas. Anger gave way to despair. I spoke a few words of appeal to Hendrick, seized my fragrant pheasant and hurriedly made for the open veld. When I returned, half an hour later, the ghoonyas and the strangers had disappeared. I never enquired as to how Hendrick had disposed of them.

After darkness had fallen I took my kaross and strolled down to the water's edge. There I spent some peaceful, contemplative hours waiting for the sea-cows which, however, did not come. Then, with a contented heart I welcomed the touch of the wing of sleep upon my eyelids, and turned over to compose my tired thews for recuperative repose against the fatigues of the morrow.

Just before dawn I woke up cold and very damp. A thick fog had rolled in with the westerly breeze. My kaross was soaked through. So dense was the vapour that I had to wait, shivering, until it was broad daylight before attempting to find my way back to the camp. Even then I had to bend down and trace, step by step, my spoor of the previous night.

Hendrick, who brought no blanket, cowered miserably over a few inadequate embers. He was wet through. The fuel collected when we camped had been all consumed. The candle-bush—that boon to travellers in Bushmanland—does not grow in the coast desert. I roused up the guides and ordered them out for fatigue duty in the form of collecting firewood. They attempted to shift the responsibility to Flora and Fauna, but I sternly repudiated this. The men, one and all, had to turn out. Flora was young; she could accompany them, but the venerable Fauna might, if she so desired, stay behind and keep the fading embers alive. I assigned to her a duty—she had to become a fog-horn for the occasion. She was ordered to shout at intervals and continuously bang one of our two tin pannikins on our only tin plate. This would prevent any members of the scattered contingent getting lost. So dense was the fog that objects were invisible at the distance of a yard.

Soon we had a roaring fire. As we would reach Arris that afternoon, I used up all the remaining coffee in a general treat. Hendrick's pannikin was the only one available for use in the distribution of the precious fluid, so after regaling Fauna first and then Flora, the four men drew lots to determine who was to drink next. The last man claimed the grounds as his perquisite. His claim was disputed, but after carefully weighing the circumstances, I decided in his favour.

Soon the wind dropped and the mist thinned out. We made a start and, after walking for about an hour, reached a camp. It comprised an ancient wagon of the wooden-axle type, a mat-house and a small goat-kraal full of stock. The establishment belonged to the most well-to-do man in the Richtersveld. He was pointed out to me as such sitting among the members of the Raad. I then noticed that he wore a good pair of breeches and an air of prosperity. This man was the local representative of Capital. He was the possessor of a pony—a creature hardly as big as a middling-sized donkey.

I enquired about game. Yes, there were springbuck in the vicinity—not more than two or three miles from the camp, and not far from out of our course to Arris. They were said to be comparatively tame. Probably they had acquired a contempt for the Richtersveld guns, which, I fancied, were of an antiquated type.

I hired the pony for the day. My principal reason for doing this was to save my boots, which were rapidly wearing out. Flora, Fauna and Flora's husband were loaded up with the baggage and sent on to Arris. Hendrick, the three remaining guides, the Capitalist owner of the pony and I went to look for the springbuck.

Our course lay south-west. The fog had receded but not disappeared; it hung more or less thickly over the plains before us. But it lifted and fell in a most peculiar way; slow undulations, and graceful, deliberate eddies played along its indefinite fringe. Soon we noticed game spoor. Yes,—the Capitalist was right. But how large the spoor was; it suggested blesbuck rather than springbuck.

What was that looming through the fog-fringe? It looked almost as large as a cow. But the brown stripe and the lyre-formed horns shewed up clearly every now and then; the creature was indubitably a springbuck. It was not more than two hundred yards away. I supposed it was the changing drift of vapour that distorted and magnified the animal. However, I fired and it fell.

When we approached the struggling creature I gazed upon it with astonishment; it was so immense. Why, it must have been nearly twice as large as the springbuck of the desert. I asked the Capitalist if this were not an extraordinary specimen. No, he said, all the bucks in the vicinity were about as large. Then I recalled having read in Francis Galton's book that he shot a springbuck weighing a hundred and sixty pounds near Walfish Bay. These Richtersveld bucks,—so the Capitalist informed me, do not trek. They must belong to a distinct sub-species,—the range of which is restricted to the Coast Desert.

As we wandered on towards Arris, the fog-curtain kept ascending and again settling down. But it did not lift to any great extent; one could never see farther than from three to four hundred yards ahead. I shot three more bucks; all were of the same type. One young animal, with horns not more than a hands-breadth long, which I shot by mistake when the fog was more than usually thick, was larger than the ordinary buck of the inland desert. I presented one of the four bucks to the Capitalist; he hid it among some bushes, intending to pick it up as he returned from Arris with the pony. The other three carcases we took on with us. I meant to cut one up and divide it among the guides. It would not have done to have left the carcase to be dismembered on the return journey; these people were so jealous of each other that a fight would surely have resulted.

We reached Arris late in the afternoon. I learnt that some people had been there with ghoonyas, but Fauna so terrified them with a description of my wrath on the occasion of the last gatherers turning up, that they fled. To prevent misunderstanding it had better be explained that Arris is not a city—not even a hamlet. It is merely a place where, in specially favourable seasons, a few of the Richtersvelders sojourn with their goats. The locality is usually known by another name; one that is more realistic than refined.

Andries had rather chafed under the delay. Not knowing that springbuck were to be found in the vicinity he undertook the suggested expedition to the mouth of the Orange River, but turned back on account of the dense fog. However, he saw what I should dearly love to have seen: a troop of those wild horses which roam over that section of the desert.

He had been walking along the river shore about ten miles from here when the fog partially lifted. Within about two hundred yards of him he saw eight shaggy horses with long, flowing manes and tails. They at once plunged into the water and swam out to the celebrated islands—that forest-covered archipelago which there enriches the river's widened course. I much regretted having missed that sight. Descended as they are from tame animals which escaped from man's control, these horses are as wild as the oryx. They have so far evaded capture by invariably taking to the water when pursued, and seeking refuge in the extensive island labyrinth. Long may they continue to do so.

The hour had now arrived for disbanding my corps of guides. I think I may truthfully say that we parted with genuine mutual esteem. The carcase of one of the springbuck had been dismembered and divided by lot among the faithful six. Pay had been distributed; likewise tobacco. I delivered a valedictory address.

With evident reluctance these people picked up their portions of meat and prepared to depart. Fauna apparently desired to communicate with me privately; she stood apart and gazed with appeal in her eyes. I went to her; she asked in a low, nervous voice—speaking in much-broken Dutch—if I would not send her some of the medicine made from the reptiles and insects which had been collected.

At length I caught the drift of her meaning: she thought I was about to prepare from these ingredients some philtre that would bring back vanished youth. Truly, the mind of man is one when the crust of convention is pierced. This poor old creature, like Ponce de Leon, dreamt of Bimini and longed for a return of the thrilling ecstasies of life's morning. It cut me to the heart to have to shatter the fabric of her dream.

We decided to start for home on the following morning. I was sorry not to be able to visit the Orange River mouth and its flamingo-haunted dunes—the Vigita Magna of the old geographers. Strange, that I should again have had to miss it when only a few miles away. But I was really pressed for time; other duties insistently called me hundreds of miles thence. Nevertheless, had it not been for the fog, I would have expended another day. But the fog towards the coast was denser than ever, and there did not appear to be any reasonable likelihood of its clearing. So I would forego the barren privilege of being able to say that I had actually visited Vigita Magna.

Our homeward course lay more to the westward, for we travelled along the coast until close to Port Nolloth. We found fresh water at various spots, trickling out of sand hummocks in the immediate vicinity of the sea. We had a comparatively easy journey, for there were no steep, rocky ridges to cross.

Chapter Thirteen.

Kamiebies—The Blossoming Wilderness—The Ostrich Poachers—Hail Storms—The Springbuck behind the Dune—How Andries found me.

Reliable information reached me to the effect that the Half-Breed ostrich poachers had again been at their nefarious work. So we decided, Andries and I, to make a swoop upon the camp which these people had established in southern Bushmanland. This camp was in the vicinity of some wells, the water of which was brackish to such an extent that only men or animals who had gradually accustomed themselves to its flavour and properties, could consume it. Thus the gang of poachers had for a long time been able to defy us. After rain, however, the water grew somewhat less brackish. On the rare occasions when rain fell heavily, the proportion of brack decreased so much that the water became, for a few weeks, more or less fit for ordinary consumption.

The reason was a phenomenal one; the rains had set in a month before their usual time throughout the western desert and the mountain tract. It was then the end of March, and rain had been falling, off and on, for the previous fortnight. Rarely, indeed, did the drought break before the middle of April.

There was also news of the springbucks. The great migration was not due to take place for months, but word had reached Andries to the effect that in the desert somewhere to the east of Kamiebies a moderately large herd had been seen. If the news were true, that herd must have been the first wave of an early-coming tide. Thus we might be able to settle accounts with the poachers and provide our year's supply of "bultong" in the course of one expedition.

The annual migration of springbucks across the desert is, I am positive, an institution of immemorial antiquity. The reason for it is obvious. The fawns are

79

born in winter, and it is necessary that at the time the does should have green food to eat. But Bushmanland, excepting its extreme western fringe, is far drier in winter than in summer. In winter the feathery plumes of the "toa" crumble away to dust and the stumps of the tussocks turn jet-black. Then the plains become unmitigated desert.

Winter is the season during which rain falls among the mountains lying between Bushmanland and the coast desert. Then for a few short weeks the mountain range covers itself with verdure and flowers. Therefore the trek. However, of late years the mountain tract has been largely taken up by farmers, so the springbuck, as a rule, invade only its eastern margin. The western fringe of the plains usually get a slight sprinkling from the mountain rains. The exception happens when the trek, instead of being distributed over a wide extent, concentrates. Then the springbuck, in their myriads, over-run hundreds of square miles of the mountain tract, and clear the face of the country of vegetation as completely as would a swarm of locusts.

The term "springbuck" is not a satisfying one for this ethereal creature—this most lovely and graceful of the animals whose home is in the desert. The name is too obvious; why not call it what it really is, a "gazelle?" But the early Dutch inhabitants of South Africa not alone lacked imagination, but shewed positive ineptitude in the names they bestowed on the various wild animals. Take for instance the term "gemsbok," as applied to the oryx; what could be more inappropriate? "Gemsbok" means "Chamois"—and we have in South Africa an antelope which is a chamois to all intents and purposes, but which is called a "klipspringer." Again,—the tall, heavy, sober-tinted desert bustard is called the "paauw," a word which means "peacock." However, these names are so firmly fixed in the South African vocabulary that any endeavour to change them would be a hopeless task.

We trekked south-east from Silverfontein in the spring-wagon, behind a team of eight spanking horses. We slept at Kamiebies, which is an uncertain water-place a few miles over the edge of the desert and a short day's journey south of Gamoep. During the day we rested; in the night we had to make a dash of some forty miles for our objective. We meant to take the poachers by surprise,—to drop on them just at daybreak, as though from the clouds. So in the mean time I lazed through the long, delicious day.

The rains had not alone been earlier and heavier than usual, but they had fallen throughout an unusually extensive area. The mountain tract was ablaze with flowers; even Bushmanland stirred in its aeon-old sleep, for the skirts of the last rain-cloud had trailed well over its borders, and the latent life of the waste had leaped, responsive, to the surface. Now a whole flora that had slept for years in tubers and dry stalks sent forth blossoms in million-fold rivalry to attract the replete, drowsy insects.

Here, from a dense, thorny, involuted mass of gnarled, shapeless stems that must have been many centuries old, arose the delicate, fairy-like petals of a scented pelargonium. The corolla was snow-white, except for a minute, sagittate marking of bright cerise on the lower lip. If you had examined ten thousand of these flowers you would not have found one in which that little mark varied to the extent of the ten-thousandth part of an inch. The thought of which that blossom was the manifestation—the afterthought of which the tiny cerise arrowhead was the expression—dwelt down in the unlovely labyrinth of the monstrous stems, and had been adhered to with steady persistence through successions of long arid-year periods. It was whispered to the silk-winged seed from which that hoary patriarch had birth,—perhaps when Alaric was thundering at the gates of Rome. And it would be as unerringly transmitted to blossoms making sweet the breeze in days when men will hold this generation to be as remote as we hold the dwellers of the Solutrè Cavern.

There swayed a slender heliophila—the modest sunlover who, in the course of age-long, patient vigils, had drawn down and ensnared the hue of the desert sky in her petals. Far and near the plain was starred with beauty. The small, inornate, thirst-land butterflies had ventured out from the hills; they flitted to and fro, lazy and listless. They sported with Amaryllis in the sunshine and then tried to flirt shamelessly with Iris, the shy maiden on the nodding, hair-like stem—who veiled her visage in sober brown by day, but revealed it, white and eager to the stars whilst she made the wings of the night-wind faint with perfume.

An oval shrub attracted one's attention—not through its beauty, but because it was an object startling and bizarre. It looked as though covered with rags of various tints. This was that criminal among vegetables—the Roridula. A close inspection almost filled one with horror; the plant was like a shambles. The leaves resembled toothed traps; in most of them insects were tightly gripped. After these had been sucked dry,—drained of blood and of every vestige of bodily juices, the leaves opened, dropped the mangled and dessicated frames to the ground and cynically opened their fell jaws for more victims. Undeterred by the litter of corpses that cumbered the surrounding ground, other insects crowded in to taste of the viscid juice which the leaves exuded. This was the bait tempting to their doom moths, butterflies, beetles and other minor fauna. Here was Capitalism playing on the greed and credulity of the crowd,—gorging on the life-blood of its hapless dupes,—flourishing and waxing strong amid the ruin of its countless victims.

My eye was caught by a quivering twig; on it was a chameleon. The reptile was nearly nine inches long. His colour was brown, of a shade exactly the same as that of the twig. He moved forward with slow, hesitating steps; he paced like an amateur on the tight-rope, as though afraid of falling. His swivel eye-cases, each with a tiny, diamond-bright speck in the centre, moved about independently of each other. One was focussed on a little green insect waving its antennae on a leaf six inches in front of him; the other was carefully trained backwards over his left shoulder at me. Flick—and his tongue shot out and in so rapidly that the eye could hardly follow its motion. But the insect was no longer on the leaf, and the chameleon was munching something with solemn enjoyment. When night fell he would climb to the top of a strong, dry twig, roll and tuck himself into the shape of a pear, with his head in the centre of the bulge. Then he would change his hue to white and open his mouth, which was bright orange internally. The night-flying lepidoptèra would take him for a white, yellow-centred flower, and pop in, seeking nectar. But they would not pop out again.

And the greatest wonder of all,—I bent down to examine a gazania; its inch-long golden rays expanded like a wheel of perfect symmetry. Just where the ray bent over the edge of the green, fleshy cup in which the myriad florets were nested, was a small, dark spot. I brought a simple magnifying glass to bear on this,—and what did I see? A labyrinthine crater of many-coloured fire opened. Curve melted and mingled into reluctant curve, zone into rainbow zone, until the plummet of vision was lost in the radiant abyss. I lifted the flower gently; its texture was thinner than the thinnest paper; beneath it was the desert sand. It had hardly any material thickness, yet infinity lay in its depths. I sought for a gazania of another species and found its petals eyed like the peacock's tail. Yet another,—it shewed the rose-ardours of dawn contending with the purple of a sea on whose surface night still brooded. Every species had its own colour-scheme—its maze of splendour more intricate than the labyrinth of King Minos.

Old Mr Von Schlicht of Klipfontein—who had spent most of his life in Namaqualand, had recently been endeavouring to recall for me details of the desert journeys of Ecklon and Drege, who did so much for South African botany. I ascertained that Ecklon visited Kamiebies. How his heart must have leaped when his eyes first gathered in the winter glory of those mountains. When he afterwards stood, begging his bread at the corner of the Heerengracht, Cape Town,—did he ever recall that scene? Strange world of men that so often lets its noblest, after lives of heroic toil for the highest and most unselfish ends, die in the gutter—if it does not more mercifully slay them—and pays tribute of corn, wine and oil, of jewels and fine raiment, to the company-monger or other chartered robber adroit enough to squeeze through the meshes of the law.

We inspanned at sunset, and plunged straight into the desert, travelling slightly to the south of east. Our objective was lower Pof Adder—which must not be confounded with the northern Pof Adder beyond Namies. We were out of the region of "toa"; the plain was covered with small shrub,—half of which were soft and succulent and the others hard and thorny. There were no intermediate kinds; the desert is a region of extremes.

In spite of the jolting I managed to get a few hours' sleep. We outspanned for an hour at midnight and made coffee. Now we had some heavy sand-tracts to cross,—with jolty stretches lying between them. But we reached the camp of the half-breeds just at dawn, as had been intended.

They were caught—if not exactly red-handed, yet with ample proof of their guilt. In the mat-houses of the suspected men we found boxes and bags packed full of feathers. These were of all kinds—from the long white plumes and the short blacks of the male bird, to the browns of the hens and chicks. The culprits pleaded guilty; retributive justice was forthwith satisfied at the wagon-wheel.

The camp was quite a large one; I should say it contained over sixty souls, men, women and children included. These people were all of the same colour, light-yellow; they even seemed to shew signs of type-inception. Lean, sinewy and tough, they were not beautiful either in form or feature. In neither sex did the sallow skin give any hint of blood beneath. However, anaemic as they were, whatever fluid circulated in their arteries must have been of good quality, for their capacity for physical endurance was considerable.

It was the eyes of those half-breeds that were most distinctive. These were dusky and deep, with an expression—not exactly furtive; rather expressive of haunting apprehension. This was hardly to be wondered at, for they had ceaselessly to watch for every change in the desert's pitiless visage—to note each alteration in the moods of earth and sky. Their lives were spent in answering a succession of riddles propounded by the terrible sphinx between whose taloned paws they existed as playthings.

Their dwellings—ordinary mat-houses and ramshackle wagons—as well as the furniture thereof, indicated that they must have become habituated to extremes of heat and cold. They were cleanly in their persons; this I knew through having vaccinated them all,—from the patriarch to the youngest baby. Small-pox at the time was reported to be raging among the Bondleswartz Tribe, just beyond the Orange River.

But these people can never develop a type that will persist; the desert they inhabit is too small. Besides, their sons and daughters are continually being enticed away to regions with a kinder soil and a less severe climate. There they further complicate the South African race question. This question will not be confined to South Africa; it will soon be one of worldwide import, and one that is not necessarily to be answered in favour of the Caucasian, whose birth-rate statistics read like Mene Tekel. I am often inclined to think it would have been better in the long run had Charles Martel lost the Battle of Tours. In that case there would at all events have been no colour question.

But those deep, dusky eyes haunted me. They were as enigmatic as the only landscape over which they ranged. If one could only have stripped the scales from them, what wonders might they not have seen? Incalculable potencies might have been in their depths. Others, desert-bred, have caught glimpses of eternal verities which prompted them to utter words that became the hinges of history. However, up to the present, there is no sign of a prophet arising in Bushmanland with a message for a land that sorely needs it.

The half-breeds had heard of the springbuck; a few days previously the latter were credibly reported to be somewhere about thirty miles to the northward, near Kat Vley. And we were assured of the almost incredible fact that Kat Vley contained water. That was certainly an *annus mirabilis* in the desert.

At midday we took our departure, making for the vicinity where the springbuck were said to be. In the afternoon dense clouds rolled up from the south-westward and a deluge of hail struck us. Within the memory of men no similar thing had happened in Bushmanland. Andries and I were comfortable enough in the wagon; Hendrick and Piet Noona fixed a sail to the windward wheels and lit a big candle-bush fire to leeward. After travelling about twenty miles we had camped for the night, for the hail-clouds had been rolling up at intervals of about half an hour, and there appeared to be no likelihood of the weather clearing. The poor horses,—they were in for a time of misery!

Morning broke with drifting clouds and a high wind from the south-west. We inspanned and altered our course slightly to the westward. The hail showers had been so heavy that all spoor was obliterated; accordingly we could not tell whether game was about or not. The day was bitterly cold; over and over again the hail showers recurred. Several times we got so perished that we halted and lit fires of candle-bush just to thaw our hands at. Night fell with a slight improvement in the weather; the wind dropped and only a thin drizzle was falling. We camped again and gave the horses a liberal feed of corn. They did not appear to suffer much from the cold. Such weather was the very last thing one could have expected. But surely the sky would be clear on the morrow.

Again a cloudy morning, but the clouds were high and there was no rain. At last we saw signs of game, for we crossed the spoor of several small troops of springbuck; these had apparently been making in the direction of Kamiebies. Later we found more spoor—that of a really considerable herd making due westward.

The desert here was not quite so flat as usual; the brown expanse undulated in long, low ridges running parallel to our course. These were often several miles apart and in the spaces between, narrow sand-dunes, flat-topped and steep, extended indefinitely, east and west. At about three in the afternoon we again struck spoor. It was apparently that of the large herd whose track we had crossed a few hours previously. Now it led north-east, straight over the dune about a mile away on our right—the dune parallel to which we had been travelling for upwards of an hour. The spoor was quite fresh; it could not have been more than half an hour since the herd had passed.

We halted and outspanned. After the horses had indulged in a roll Andries and I saddled up. We rode on the spoor; soon this led us almost due north, straight to the dune, which it crossed at right angles. The herd had evidently been stampeded; it was clear they had been at a run when they passed. Their hoofs had struck deep into the wet soil and there was a distinct series of wide gaps in the dune where the crossing had been effected. We dismounted and clambered up the steep sand-slope. We looked carefully over, being heedful not to reveal ourselves. The plain before us lay empty, but about a mile to the right the herd of springbuck were visible. It was evidently one of the flying patrols of the great migratory army and apparently numbered from eight to nine thousand head.

We remounted and cantered along close to the base of the dune until we were abreast of the centre of the herd—only the dune separating us from it. Here Andries remained, while I rode on for about half a mile further. This brought me to a spot just ahead of the foremost of the game. It had been agreed that when I reached this spot Andries would cross the dune and open his attack. As soon as the herd was on the move, I would begin mine.

I dismounted, tied old Prince to a shrub, climbed the dune and laid myself flat on the top. Just to my left were the springbuck, grazing quietly and utterly unsuspicious of danger. They appeared to be all rams. This we expected, for most of the rams congregate in separate herds in the trek season. Some were grazing within less than two hundred yards of me.

When Andries' rifle spoke a thrill ran through the multitude. Looking to the left I saw the bucks beginning to stream in my direction, but the impulse had not yet been communicated to those at my end of the herd. Rythmically the impetus of flight developed towards me. Now all were on the move. I fired and a buck rolled over. Then I descended from the dune and ran forward into the plain.

The herd was now streaming past me from the direction in which the knell of Andries' regular bombardment sounded. The dense stream bent in its course before my advance, and for a few minutes took the form of a crescent at a distance of about four hundred yards. It was as though I were firing at a wall. Once I got my range nearly every bullet thudded. Soon the last of the stream flowed past, but its course for several hundred yards was marked by prone white and fawn forms.

Andries was busy collecting his dead at a spot about eight hundred yards away. I re-crossed the dune and led Prince over it at a flounder. Soon Andries came cantering up, his hands and arms red with the blood of the slain. He had killed eight bucks. I had had better chances and a longer innings, so my bag was larger, but I did not as yet know to what extent.

The sun was now almost down; my spoil was scattered over a large area. It was decided that I should gather up my dead, load the carcases upon Prince and convey them to where Andries had piled his. He started off to fetch the wagon. The team would now number only six, but the wagon was light, for the horses had consumed most of the grain. I loaded up three carcases and deposited them on the heap formed by those of Andries. Another load of three I also fetched. But night was rapidly falling so I could only negotiate one more load. This time I piled up four. When I reached the carcases depot there was little or no light. However, as long as it was possible to see what I was doing, I collected candle-bushes. The result, however, was lamentably meagre.

The wagon was only about four miles away—as the crow flies. But unfortunately the wagon was not a crow—and goodness only knew how far westward that wretched dune extended. However, even if it reached to Gamoep Andries would have to keep on its southern flank until he rounded the extremity. I began to feel miserably cold, for I had no jacket. To complete my misery the sky again clouded over and a thin rain commenced to fall.

I tied old Prince to a bush and removed his saddle. But means of the latter I should, at all events, be able to protect my neck and shoulders from the wet. Then I sat on the ground among the carcases and piled them around me; only my head emerged from the mass. The whole lot, numbering eighteen, were requisitioned for this unusual service. The water trickled in but the dead bucks still retained some heat and for a time I was fairly comfortable.

But as the hours passed the carcases grew cold and colder; my misery became acute. The night was pitch black. I had enough candle-bush to make a flare for about half-an-hour, but prudence prompted me to delay this operation so as to give Andries time to get round the extremity of the dune—wherever that might be. I fired my rifle occasionally, but the wind was blowing steadily and Andries' course was down to windward.

At length, after a seemingly interminable period of wretchedness, I lit my candle-bush flares one by one. They blazed brightly and gave out a certain amount of grateful heat, but soon they came to an end, and I stole back to my sepulchre among the now stone-cold carcases.

The steady rain trickled down; I was by this time wet through. I wondered as to whether I would be able to endure the misery until morning. I had quite made up my mind that Andries would not be able to find me. The night was too black; there were no hills nor other salient landmarks to guide him to the spot. Looking to westward before we started I could see that the dune was full of forks and branches in that direction. I tried to comfort myself with anticipation of the enormous candle-bush fire I would make as soon as day broke, and the breakfast of broiled springbuck liver I would consume. My matches were safe in a waterproof pouch. How leaden-footed is time when one is miserable!

An earth-tremor; a telephone-message thrilling along the earth's sensitive surface—telling of hoofs and wheels in rythmic motion. Had the miracle happened? Yes,—the wagon rolled up and my martyrdom was at an end. *Deo gratias*!

But how did Andries manage it? He heard no shot, he saw none of my flares. He could not tell me; as a matter of fact he, himself, did not know. His feat could only be explained through some theory of unconscious cerebration. Andries was elderly, stout and somewhat lethargic, he had never read any book but the Bible, and of that there was quite a lot he did not understand. But the trackless desert was to him as familiar as my study was to me, and he had been able to pilot his wagon-ship straight to that spot—through the inky darkness—with as little uncertainty as though the sun had been shining. The experience of a lifetime would not have taught me to perform that marvel which Andries did quite as a matter of course.

Chapter Fourteen.

L'Envoi.

My eyes have gazed their last upon the face of the desert. Although I love her still,—although the memory of her burning ardour, her splendid indifference and her wealth of illusive charm is my abiding and most valued possession, we shall meet no more. She is not a mistress to be lightly courted. As Brunhild slew Siegfried so would the Desert inevitably slay one who remained her lover after desire had outlasted strength. Her lioness-like caresses are not for those whose blood slows down as it nears the ocean of eternal silence—even as the force and fury of the Gariep sink to tranquillity when the mighty stream nears the Atlantic—and extinction.

Good-bye, Andries,—best of comrades. I have not told of all our adventures—of how we pursued the springbuck at full gallop across the trackless plains in your springless, home-made rattletrap, behind four wild, half-trained horses,—until we were black and blue. I have not told of how we were lured by men who desired our death to a spot sixty miles deep in the waste, and of how we had to struggle back again in the burning heat because we found the promised water to be brine, and the edges of the pools containing it thickly caked with salt. I have not told of your consistent unselfishness in giving me the best chances in the matter of shooting, nor of how generously you placed the riches of your desert lore at my disposal.

The world for us is not the same as it was—even a few years ago, for at our time of life a very few years make a considerable difference where physical endurance is concerned. Although on the verge of middle life we could still, in the days I have told of, gallop ten miles at a stretch and hold a rifle straight at the end of the race—we could endure thirst, hunger and fatigue without wilting.

In the matter of shooting I am, perhaps, like the reformed rake who coined virtue out of inability further to sin. Nevertheless, I could no longer take pleasure in slaughtering the few of Nature's lovely wild creatures that survive our cruelly scientific machines of precision. It is true my eyesight is not quite what it was. To what extent this circumstance should be reckoned as a factor towards my abstention, I will not attempt to say.

We shall soon be old, you and I; in fact it is almost stretching a point to call ourselves still only middle-aged. We are just a couple of ineffective veterans who can only draw comfort from the bank of our experiences. *Aber "wir haben geloebt und geliebet."*

Good-bye, Hendrick. No more will your keen and faithful eyes hold my vagrant spoor over sand and kanya. No more shall I see your bullet-shaped, pepper-corned head with its oblique eyes and gleaming teeth arising unexpectedly from among the tussocks. For all I know you may have saved me from a dreadful death. I can recall at least one occasion on which I was positively sure you were wrong in your idea as to the direction in which the camp lay,—yet the event proved you to be right. Had I then been alone, my bones might now be lying white in the heart of Bushmanland.

And you, Typhon,—I suppose you have awakened to wrath—that your hunched shoulders have heaved many times since that day on which my awed eyes beheld your russet mane flung streaming southward on the tempest,—I suppose your impotent tentacles still strive to gather up the plains into their blighting grip.

Sometimes, when the firmament is very clear and the fingers of the wind stray gently through the tresses of the night, I lift my eyes to the familiar stars and realise that again the sky has gathered the throbbing desert to its breast and covered Bushmanland with the folds of its purple mantle. It is then I unlock my storehouse of dreams and live once more through vanished days of strenuous effort and nights of wonderful mystery.

The End.

CPSIA information can be obtained at www.ICGtesting.com
Printed in the USA
BVOW06s1413170516

448427BV00016B/131/P